WOLF MAGIC

WHYCHOOSE HALLOWEEN WITCHES
BOOK THREE

AMELIA SHAW

PROLOGUE

TIFFANY

Halloween Eve.
One year and two months before.

I'd been counting down the days to this night ever since we found Sherie's spell book all those years ago. Day one thousand and ninety-five had finally arrived! My twenty-first birthday and the night I'd looked forward to for *so* long.

Tonight, on Halloween, my friends and I would cast a spell that would save us from the devastation and loneliness which had followed our mothers around like a curse their whole lives.

"So, are we going to do this, or not?" Ruby asked, then stared at Bella and me individually. "Because there's no going back after this."

Her grin made me clap my hands together with glee and a ferocious sense of determination filled me. *I never want to go back after this. I want my soul mate more than anything!*

Growing up fatherless, the only children to three heartbroken witches, had been hard on us all. So, years ago, when Ruby found an ancient spell book her mother had buried under the stairs—carefully hidden beneath blankets and tucked away within a huge chest filled with clothes and other books—we'd read it.

Of course, we had. What teenage girls wouldn't have? Ruby had led the charge, and I'd been right behind her. I needed to know why a book had been so well hidden. Inside its pages we'd found an incantation that seemed to imply a guarantee that we could avoid the heartbreak of our mothers before us. I'd been the first one of us to voice my intention. "Hell yes! This is for us!" I said.

I hadn't wanted to wait. At eighteen, I was already working, had endured one terrible fail of a romantic night, and was ready for the man of my dreams to love me so that we could build a beautiful future together.

But Bella being typical bookworm Bella had done some research and realized that the spell was complicated and required a serious amount of power to successfully pull off, which was why all three of us would need to do it. *Together.* We decided that when we were old enough, and powerful enough, we'd make it happen come hell or high water.

The wind moved through the trees around us, rustling the leaves. A fall storm was coming. I shivered at the feeling of perfect premonition as it slid over me. This was it! *We are finally here!* About to do what we'd planned and talked about for so long.

The little house in the woods that Bella's family owned was the perfect location for secret nights and escapades like this one. No one would be able to see us, and as long as we all kept our mouths shut, nobody would know that on this Halloween night, our joint twenty-first birthday, we conducted a spell to call our true loves to us.

I nodded at Ruby fiercely. It was time to start the spell—it was now or never.

Fear flashed in Bella's eyes.

Ruby sighed. "Come on, Bella. You know we can't do this without you."

And she meant that quite literally, unfortunately. Bella was by far the strongest of us and the best at spell craft. She spent an inordinate amount of her time with her nose buried in books, which was probably why.

Damn it, Bella. Don't give up on us now.

Ruby pouted, narrowing her gaze on our friend. "Come on, Bella. *Please.*"

I bit my lower lip and tried not to worry. We'd been talking about this spell for years, planning every part of this night. And now that it was here, I couldn't bear to see our one chance to slip away. I opened my mouth to beg her not to chicken out, but she spoke first, and I breathed a sigh of relief.

"Okay, Ruby. I'm in. Let's do this."

I reached for Ruby's and Bella's free hands, forming a triangle of magic and perfect strength. These girls were my family, my best friends, and the closest I'd ever get to having real sisters.

I gripped their hands tighter and stared down at the ancient book that lay on the ground between us, the spell book Ruby had found all those years ago. Excitement skittered through me, but I pushed it down. It was time to focus on getting the spell right, not get overly excited about the outcome. *Horse before the cart!* I reminded myself. If we did this properly, we could enjoy all the excitement in the world— later.

Together, we began to chant in an ancient language that no-one used anymore, a magical dialect which had been long lost to time and memory.

I concentrated hard on my lines, reading from the book. Each verse of the spell called to the magic that rippled in our veins—to Fate—and most of all, to the unconditional love that we all so desperately desired and craved.

The spell began to hurt in a way I hadn't initially expected, and I frowned at the pain, focusing on the magic we were creating, and not the headache which pounded in my temples.

My legs began to shake. *No!* I locked my knees with grim determination, not willing to give in when we were so close. Maybe Bella was right, and this spell really was too big for us to handle... I clenched my hands into fists, willing myself to greater strength. The pain started to alleviate. I smiled with satisfaction and forged forward, reading faster, loving the swirl of magic which floated around us, bonding us together more tightly than we were before.

After tonight, we'd never end up like our mothers—abandoned and alone. And for that certainty I would pay any price.

The ancient book floated in the space between us, glowing and powerful. I watched the phenomenon with a growing sense of dread but grinned in spite of it. *We're doing it. This is actually freaking happening!*

Buoyed on, we began to chant louder, the words in our hearts building naturally as the spell came to a great crescendo. White light shone between our clenched fingers and power surged through us. I gripped Ruby's and Bella's hands harder. We were almost there.

We recited the final words of the spell and the white magic we'd conjured shot into the air above our heads with a cosmic *boom*, exploding in a spectacular eruption of color, like fireworks, sparkling against the dark night sky.

We were blown backward and apart by the power of the spell, our joined hands separating as we sailed through the air.

I landed hard on my ass on the dewy grass—the magic gone in an instant as it quickly dissipated. I shook my head, pushing my hands into the ground to hold myself up. *Whoa. That was so much more intense than I expected.*

"Is that it?" Ruby asked from about ten feet away.

The spell book that had been hovering in the air between us, landed in the dirt with a heavy thump, the cover closing of its own accord.

I jumped up, brushing the dirt from my pants as happiness flowed through me. We'd done it! Now, we just had to wait for our soul mates to find us. When they did, I'd have a husband. *And kids!* And a home filled with laughter and fun. I'd have everything I never did growing up. Tears gathered in my eyes, and I blinked them back. I couldn't believe it. We'd really finished the spell. My life-long wish was about to come true.

Ruby rose from her spot on the ground.

Bella got to her feet, too.

I closed my eyes and tilted back my head, breathing in the cool night air as the stars shimmered above. This was the start of the rest of my life. Now, I just had to exercise a little bit of patience, which was definitely going to be the hard part. I wanted my soul mate, now!

"So... back to the house for a celebratory drink?" Ruby asked, dusting off her hands.

Absolutely! "Sounds like a plan," I said, flicking my long blonde hair over my shoulder.

We turned and trekked back to the house. Once inside, we turned on the lights and Ruby used her magic to mix us up some cocktails the colors of the sunset—red, orange, and yellow, with a splash of dusky purple.

"Perfect," Ruby said as she picked up her glass that had been resting on the counter.

Bella and I plucked up our drinks as well and clinked them with Ruby's.

"Happy birthday, ladies," we chorused together, grinning as a group.

The best part of my birthday was getting to spend it with these two girls.

We all took a sip of our first legal drink and grimaced at the sheer amount of liquor Ruby had poured into our mix.

I gasped, my nose burning.

"Wow, that's strong," I said, blinking rapidly to clear my eyes, before I took another sip just for good measure.

Bella inhaled sharply and coughed, then waved her hand over the table in front of us, conjuring up a veritable feast of savory and sweet snacks. Chips, chocolate cake, cookies, and crackers with cheese littered the surface in front of us.

"Oh, perfect. Thanks, Belle!" Ruby said, grabbing a handful of chips and stuffing them in her mouth.

I took another sip of my drink. The alcohol warmed my belly and filled me with a nice, relaxed feeling.

"What's up, Bell-Bell?" Ruby asked.

I glanced between them. Was something wrong? What had I missed?

"Do you think it worked?" Bella asked quietly.

Ruby shrugged. "I don't know. I hope so. I mean, I guess we'll find out."

"I hope so too!" I said, my tone exasperated. "We've only been planning this since forever."

The other two sat down with me, around our tasty birthday spread on stools Ruby had conjured out of thin air. We chatted and ate, drank and laughed, celebrating the fact we had our whole lives ahead of us.

"What do you think your guy will look like?" I asked, directing my question to Ruby, being that Bella was sitting there looking like she was about to fall asleep.

Ruby laughed. "I really don't care, as long as he's nice."

"Nice? *Pah!*" I said, rolling my eyes. "I want my guy to be *hot*. With blue eyes, and massive muscles. A ripped six-pack..."

We talked all night and finally fell asleep sometime before dawn. I was the last to pass out because I was the most excited by far.

Ruby was still a little lost with what she wanted out of life.

Meanwhile, Bella was at college and had her sights set on a career.

I'd already been working full time for three years and was *so* done with being single it wasn't funny. I wanted my man. I wanted a baby.

For me, the time until I found my soul mate couldn't pass quickly enough. Surely because of that, I'd be the first one to find my man...

· CHAPTER 1

TIFFANY

I stepped into Ruby's new backyard and stroked my dad's fluffy head, running my fingers through the gray fur with a sigh. I was impressed with the health of his thickening pelt. He was healing so well since coming home and living at Jackson's house, no longer exiled to the wild and fending for himself.

"I brought you guys some chicken and vegetables," I announced as I walked over to the porch and laid out the supplies from my basket I'd brought. Mom had sent me with Tupperware tubs full of delicious, warm food. Something our fathers had no doubt missed—being condemned to their wolf forms—since our mothers fell pregnant with us.

I laid out three porcelain plates and served their food before stepping back to stare at their lunch. I hated the fact that our fathers had to be fed like, well, dogs. But until we found a way to break the spell, there was nothing for it but to deal.

I sat down on the porch step.

Two of the wolves stepped forward and began to eat their meals.

But my father stared at me, seeming almost embarrassed.

I didn't really know how he felt, but I could guess. I don't think he liked me watching him eat like a common mutt. "Can I feed you, Dad?" I offered.

The gray wolf shifter that was my father, a man I'd never actually met in the flesh, crouched down in front of me.

I picked up the plate I'd set out for him, took a piece of cooked chicken breast and held it out to him.

He took the meat carefully from my fingers and gulped it down.

The other two wolves were practically inhaling their lunch.

Poor things. So, I kept feeding my father, holding piece after piece out to him until the need to speak into the silence overwhelmed me. "You're going to think I'm so vain for saying this, but I literally have no-one else to talk to," I said. It was a strange admission for me. Once upon a time I'd considered myself the luckiest girl alive, to have two best friends who were closer to me than sisters. I'd always been able to tell them anything. But things were different now, and in that moment, I'd never felt so alone.

My dad tilted his large wolf head in a way that I took to mean, 'go for it'.

I smiled and went on. "I'm so... angry, Dad. Like... *all* the time. I don't know what to do about all these stupid feelings rolling around inside me. It feels like a storm! I shouldn't be mad, but I'm just so... lonely. And surprised to be honest. I thought I would be the first one to find my soul mate, and I still haven't found mine even though the other two have."

My dad tilted his head the other way.

I groaned. "Yeah, I know. I sound like a spoiled brat. But I don't mean to. It's just that..." I sighed. This was going to sound terrible, but I was going to say it anyway. "Everyone's always told me I'm the prettiest, the sexiest, of the three of us. You know? I'm certainly not the smartest or the kindest. But I thought that if anyone was going to find their man, or in this case, her men early, it would be me. I've been ready and waiting since my sweet sixteenth!"

That night I'd been set on losing my virginity, but the warlock I clumsily tried to seduce hadn't been 'up' to the task. For the one everyone called 'the blonde one', like I was some cheap Barbie doll, I certainly wasn't having much luck finding someone who'd have sex with me. Not that I was going to share *that* with my dad.

I was down to the mix of vegetables and the small remnants of chicken. "Here you go." I placed the plate down in front of him.

He ate the remaining food.

Then all three wolf shifters gathered near me, staring at me as though waiting for me to speak.

I sighed. "I know it sounds like I think I'm the prettiest or something, but I don't! Ruby's just beautiful. And Bella? She doesn't know it, but she's striking, no matter what she wears. It's just that... I guess I just thought someone would want me. At least as a wife. But I can't even find one mate." I took a deep breath and sighed. "Humans are scared of being with us and the warlocks have never liked us. I used to wonder why, but now that I know I'm half wolf shifter, I know why they don't find us attractive."

Humans and warlocks had one thing in common—a natural fear of wolf shifters, unless they were our mates.

"But I..." I knew I sounded like an impatient little bitch, so I stopped talking, frustrated even more now than when I'd begun. I needed to just get over myself, but I was sick of feeling like I wasn't special! I was, wasn't I? *To someone?* I stared at my father, a man who'd shifted into a wolf twenty-three years ago and had never been able to shift back.

We believed it was because of a curse the High Warlock had conjured before we were born, but we weren't totally sure about all the details. We only had our suspicions and what Tabitha had told us, but that bitch would say anything to hurt us. She would have lied about everything if it had suited her. But we would find out the truth. *Somehow.*

It saddened me to no end that my father had lost the chance to see me grow up. They'd all lost the chance to be married and have more children, or at least get to know the one daughter each of them had. And I was complaining because I was twenty-two, and still single? *At least I can eat with my hands!* I sobbed into those very hands. "I'm sorry. I'm being so childish and bitchy."

My dad put his head on my knee and growled a little.

I laughed at his expression, though there were tears in my eyes. "Who did this to you? To us?" I asked rhetorically. "I spent my whole life without a father... and I could have really used one."

Not that I was complaining about my mom. She was great. But there were times when a girl wanted a dad, though. A man to talk to. A male to give her a hug when things were rough. And for me... *now* was one of those times.

My dad moved so that he could lie on his side, then sighed heavily.

I chuckled to myself. He had such a great way of communicating, even without words.

"Hey, Tiff! I didn't realize you were here," Ruby called out from behind me, walking out the back door of her huge house.

I glanced up as she stood beside me. "Yeah. Sorry. I thought I'd deliver the food, then come in, but I got stuck talking."

Ruby grinned, her hand straying absently to her still-flat belly. "I come out here and talk to my dad all the time. We've told them to come and sleep in the lounge, but they don't seem to want to come inside, so yeah... Trying to make up for lost time, right?"

I shrugged and gestured to her belly. "How are you feeling?"

She smiled. "Just hit eight weeks and feeling violently ill most days." She laughed weakly, but I saw the truth on her face. She was pale and looked like she'd lost weight. "But I've been told it's a good sign. It means it's a strong pregnancy."

I forced myself to my feet. "Well, that's great to hear, Ruby."

My best friend was mated to three men and pregnant, and I still didn't have a boyfriend. Color me green with envy.

Ruby tilted her head at me. "What's up with you? You seem a little off."

I shook my head. "Oh, nothing." I indicated to the inside of the house. "You all ready for Christmas? Need any help with decorating or anything?"

Ruby's magic still hadn't returned, or if it had, she wasn't using it. We didn't know if it was due to the pregnancy—and her witch abilities would return after the baby was born—or if her magic was gone forever after what she'd endured last Halloween night. The night she'd fought on her own to remove the love spell we'd cast to find our soul mates in the first place.

"Come see," she said.

I waved goodbye to my dad as we walked up the stairs and into the huge house and stepped into the open plan living area. "Wow. You've gone all out," I breathed in awe. The once all-white house was now splattered with festive color. "What a tree!" I stared at the six-foot pine tree in the corner of the lounge room, lavished in gleaming gold and glittering silver baubles.

Ruby inhaled deeply. "Doesn't it smell great?"

I couldn't smell much, but assumed her heightened senses was a pregnancy thing. "Did the guys help you decorate?" I asked, glancing around at the tinsel lining the doorways, the twinkling lights, and strung-up mistletoe.

"Yeah, the old-fashioned way—with ladders, and sticky tape, and lots of cursing when everything fell down again!" She giggled. "I'm sure Mom will come by later and magic things up a bit."

Ruby's smile was infectious, and I grinned. "Most definitely." I sat down on one of the bar stools next to her large kitchen bench and sighed, my tummy growling loudly.

"Was that your stomach?" Ruby asked, pulling open the fridge door. "You want something to eat? Or drink?"

I nodded. "A drink would be great. Thanks."

Ruby poured me a soda.

I took a sip, the cold bubbles quenching some of my thirst, but not really doing much to bolster my mood.

Ruby grabbed a candy from a bowl nearby, before shoving it toward me, and popping one in her mouth. "These help with the nausea, so I need to suck them constantly."

I shrugged. "Go for it. Whatever makes you feel better." I traced an invisible pattern on the marble countertop, then stood up. "I probably should get going."

"Why? Are you working tonight?"

I was a hairdresser and had been working my ass off in the lead up to Christmas. "No, I've got the night off, thankfully. I've been doing overtime every day though, and I might need to work tomorrow." Tomorrow being Saturday, but since I'd worked all week, they'd given me Friday off. Christmas was on Monday, so at least I had a few days off after tomorrow.

"So, why are you rushing off then?"

I shrugged again, settling back down onto the stool. "You know. Just... Christmas stuff."

Ruby stared at me, her gaze searching. "What's going on with you, Tiff?"

"Nothing. What do you mean?"

Ruby rolled her eyes theatrically. "What do you mean, what do I mean? You're sad! It's so stinking obvious. Why won't you just talk openly about it? Bell and I are here for you, you know that right?"

I frowned and glared down at my hand, where my fingers still traced patterns on the marble countertop. I didn't want to admit to Ruby that she was right: I *was* sad—and lonely. I swallowed, not sure how to start that sentence.

I expected Ruby to take over the conversation like she normally did, being the life of our trio, and demand that I reveal all.

But she was pressing her hands into the counter and breathing hard like she was suddenly in pain.

I jumped to my feet, instantly alarmed. "Hey, Ruby. Are you okay?"

She was getting paler by the minute. She shook her head and stumbled sideways. "I... no..." Her eyes rolled back in her head, and she began to faint dead away to the floor.

"Ruby!" I wasn't close enough to catch her, but I threw out a spell on instinct and froze her, just inches before she hit the ground. I raced around the island and knelt, putting my arms beneath her before releasing the spell, so she fell into my waiting arms.

She was heavier than I anticipated, so I called on my magic and used a carrying spell to carefully transport her into the large bedroom on the ground floor. I pulled back the covers and used my magic to slide her into the bed, resting her head on the pillow. I dragged the covers over her and touched a hand to her cheek, then to my own face for comparison.

She was too cool, though I didn't know if that was a problem or not. Or was it only when you were too warm? I pressed my hands into my temples, a headache pounding inside my brain. "What do I do? What do I do?"

I didn't want to leave Ruby, but just sitting here and waiting for one of her mates to get home wasn't an option either. So, I pulled out my phone and checked the time. The guys wouldn't be home for hours and Bella was at college.

I stared at my cell screen and realized there was only one person I was comfortable calling. I hit the name on my favorites list and the phone began to ring. "Please pick up, please pick up," I chanted. She was at work, and I wasn't sure if she'd hear the ringtone or not. When her voice finally came through, I almost cried.

"Tiffany. What's happened?"

"Mom. You need to help me. Something's wrong with Ruby!"

CHAPTER 2

TIFFANY

Within moments of hanging up the phone, Mom used a transportation spell to get to me. After seeing the state of Ruby and deducing it came from a magical source, we didn't call the hospital. Instead, she called all the moms, and Bella. Within an hour, we had both generations together.

"Do you know what's wrong with her?" I asked Sherie, Ruby's mom, who was waving her hands over her daughter, analyzing the problem, white sparkling magic coursing over Ruby's body.

My mom stepped up next to me and squeezed my hand. "We don't know, honey. Sherie's doing a spell to stabilize Ruby, but from what we can tell the pregnancy is, um, more or less draining the life out of her."

I spun around and stared at her, aghast. "Are you telling me the baby's actually killing her?" That couldn't be true. Surely all pregnant moms felt like their life was being drained by their baby? Wasn't it said that the first trimester was always the worst?

Sherie dropped her hands and sighed, turning toward me with tears in her eyes. "Ruby's carrying a daughter, but the curse on the pack still means that no daughters are allowed to be born from this generation. Ruby's strong. She's managed so far, but I'm not sure how much longer the baby—or she—will last." Sherie bit her lip and stared at my mom, tears glistening in her scared eyes. "Do you think I should... if it would save her..."

I glanced between the two moms, trying to work out what they were referring to. When neither one spoke, and simply continued to stare at each other in long, knowing looks, I threw my hands up and said, "What are you talking about?"

Bella walked forward, a tear stain on one cheek. "They might be able to save Ruby—if they terminate the pregnancy."

"No!" I raced over to stand by Ruby who lay in the bed, helpless. She couldn't speak for herself, so I'd have to do it for her. I'd be her advocate. I knew in my heart she'd never want to end her baby's life. *Never!*

Not that I would physically be able to stop our moms if they really wanted to do it. They were much stronger than me. And ultimately, I was only half-witch, and had never really cared that much about perfecting my craft. I was a half-assed witch at the best of times. In this moment I regretted not focusing more on improving my magical skills.

But I could see how much pain was on both their faces and used that knowledge to my advantage. "You can't do it. You can't kill Ruby's baby!" I repeated. "She will never forgive you if you do."

The front door opened, and men's voices rang out throughout the house. "Ruby! You home, honey?"

"How are you feeling?" called another male voice. "Any better?"

Bella stared at the bedroom door, a look of worry on her face.

I clung to Ruby's headboard and called out, "We're in here!"

Two of Ruby's men stepped into the room, passing through one at a time.

Jackson had to turn his shoulders slightly to the side as he passed through since he was so damn big.

Darren didn't have a hope of sliding past him.

"What's going on?" Jackson asked, lingering near the doorway.

Darren hurried straight over to the bed, comfortable enough to come into the room with a full coven of witches hovering around his mate. But Darren was part-warlock, so he was always more comfortable around us than the other full-blooded wolves. Magic was a part of who he was, whether he could use it or not. "Is she okay?" Darren asked, reaching out for one of Ruby's hands and touching her fingers. "Shit, she's deathly cold."

Bella's mom, Kathy, stepped up. "We're pretty sure the pregnancy's killing her. So, we need to decide if we roll the dice and wait and see what's going to happen... or..." She let the unspoken words hang in the air.

Jackson took a step in the room. "Or, what?" he said, his voice rough with emotion. "We can't lose Ruby. I don't care what you have to do."

"We need to abort the pregnancy," Kathy said.

Darren gasped in shock and despair.

Jackson's face flashed with sharp pain, before he clenched his jaw and nodded once. "Do it."

I gasped at him. *No!* "Jackson, you don't mean that!" I turned to Darren.

He'd climbed onto the bed and was now lying down next to his mate, brushing her long red hair away from her face.

"Darren!"

He stared at me, his eyes shimmering with unshed tears. "We can't lose Ruby, Tiff. We can't. The three of us would die."

I wasn't sure if he meant it literally, but from the heavy feeling in the room, and the hardness in Jackson's face, they might. I stomped my foot, unwilling to give up. "No! Ruby will kill us if we do it! And that's assuming she even survives the process." I glared at the moms. "Can you guarantee that you can save her if you kill her baby?"

Mom glanced at Sherie. "We... can't. We don't know how tightly entwined Ruby and her daughter are with the spell. If we sever the connection, we could kill them both."

Jackson groaned and turned away, grabbing a hold of the door frame and squeezing so hard the wood cracked beneath his fingers.

I turned to Bella in desperation. Surely, she'd be on my side. "Come on, Bell! There has to be another way."

Bella chewed her lip before replying. "Well, I suppose we could do some sort of temporary stasis spell. We might be able to hold her like this for a few days. Maybe more. But any longer and you'll endanger the fetus anyway. It needs time to grow and change and keeping them like that too long will kill the baby."

"Why would you do that, then?" Darren asked from the bed.

"It would give us time to figure out what's going on," Bella said. "Maybe even find a way to break the curse once and for all."

"But you've been working on it for a month, and haven't gotten anywhere yet," Darren said, his tone thick with despair.

I wanted to shake him, shake them all. There was no way Ruby would give up this easily. If she wasn't in a coma right now, she'd slap them all silly! I glared at him. "It's the best hope we have, unless you can think of anything else that might save her?" I glanced from Darren to my mom, to Sherie, and then to Jackson.

They all shook their heads, or stared at the floor, unable or unwilling to look at me.

I took a deep breath, knowing that I was right in my determination to try and save them both. I knew that the fetus was young, and technically Ruby and her mates could try again for another baby if they saved Ruby. But she would never forgive us, or her mates, for killing her daughter. I knew my friend, and that was a certainty.

I closed my eyes and inside my mind I saw Ruby, cradling her infant daughter in her arms. She was a beautiful cherub with blonde hair and blue eyes, and my friend loved her more than anything in the world. I wasn't taking that away from her.

As I opened my eyes, tears spilled down my face as my heart ached with pain, realizing how far away from that vision we were. I brushed away the tears with haste. "We're saving them both. I don't care what we have to do. This curse was built from a place of ignorance and hatred. Surely the love you two have for your mates, and our moms have for our dads, is enough to break it!"

"It hasn't been enough so far," Bella said. "Unless the spell needs you to find your mates, too?" She smiled gently at me.

The soft joke made me sigh. "It might, but I think I've met every wolf in town now. *Twice.* My mates don't live here. Or they're not from this pack."

The room went deathly quiet, then the front door opened and closed again. "Hey, Ruby!"

Billy walked into the room wearing a leather jacket and I couldn't help the admiration that flowed through me. Of all Ruby's mates, Billy was my favorite: quiet, strong, sexy. The classic bad boy. His expression fell. "What happened?"

We filled him in, and by the time we'd finished, he was sitting on the blanket box, with his head in his hands, looking just as miserable as I felt.

"You have to save her," he said quietly, and when he looked up, his eyes flashed yellow with his wolf.

"Hey. Calm down. It's okay," Jackson said, squeezing Billy's shoulder.

Billy jumped up. "It's not okay. How are we meant to...?"

He stopped, swallowing audibly as he struggled to contain his emotions.

Bella, who in the past would have run from such a strong, emotional male, stepped closer. I watched her in admiration. Having two Alpha mates had really changed her.

"Billy. We're going to try and save both of them, but I've got a hunch that the only way we're going to break this spell is when all three of us have found our mates. Can you think of anyone that Tiffany hasn't met that she should? Or maybe she needs to meet some guys from other packs?"

"You really think us three finding our wolf shifter mates will break the curse?" I repeated. *Was Bella serious?* I crossed my arms over my chest, not liking the way they were talking about me. Like I was a problem or something. Or my singledom was part of the curse. Though if someone would point me in the right direction of my mates, I'd be grateful.

Bella nodded. "I think it's definitely a part of it. Think about what happened when I found my mates. Tabitha and David tried to kill us! The closer we get to finding love and happiness, the closer we get to destroying that spell."

I wasn't so sure about that. Tabitha had said the spell was grounded in us, but could love really break a spell that in the past we had assumed only our deaths could?

"You know I've tried everything, Bella," I grumbled. It wasn't like I hadn't tried to find my mates.

Billy jumped to his feet. "Hang on a second! I didn't even think..."

He turned to look at Jackson.

"What are you talking about?" Jackson asked.

"I was coming back to tell you I just saw Jase, Ollie, and Fin. They're home for Christmas!"

I frowned. I didn't recognize any of those names. "Who are they?"

"Do you think it's possible?" Jackson asked Billy, ignoring my question.

"Why not?" Billy said. "They're three wolf shifters. All Betas."

"They're all gray, too," Darren said from the bed.

I turned toward him. "What do you mean?" I was shaking now, and I wasn't sure why. I wasn't afraid, or cold. "What's that got to do with anything?"

"You're right!" Billy said, moving closer to the bed, excitement catching in his voice. He turned to me. "Do you remember at Thanksgiving? We were talking about the fact that all of Ruby's mates are white wolves..."

"Yeah, and all of Bella's are black." I shrugged. "And I joked that mine would be all brown..."

"Or gray!" Billy said, casting a worried look at Ruby.

I frowned. "Yeah, but you said that there weren't any gray wolves in your generation." Or he'd said they were unusual, or something like that.

Darren sat up. "They're super-rare. There are only three gray wolves in our whole pack our age, and they're three best friends, all Betas."

My heart pounded faster, a premonition-type wave flowing over me, making me shiver. "Then why haven't I met them?"

Darren glanced at Billy, who said, "Because last year they left the pack. They got frustrated at being single, and said they were going to go look for their mates, and they took off. They've been all over the country, I heard."

I bit my lip. *What if they've brought home a woman, or three?* "Do you really think they could be my mates?"

Jackson laughed. "Only one way to tell! Let's go introduce you."

I glanced at my mom, who nodded. "Go. We'll get to work on the stasis spell. See if we can hold Ruby and her baby long enough that we can break the curse that binds you all."

Bella hurried over to me. "I'll come with you. The moms can look after Ruby."

I grabbed Bella's hand. "Thanks." I needed the support, now more than ever.

The guys all stopped by the bed to kiss Ruby and whisper to her.

I tried not to listen out of respect for their privacy.

Once they were done, they charged out the door and Bella and I followed— hopefully to fulfil a date with destiny!

· CHAPTER 3 ·
OLIVER

I leaned back in the café booth, stretched my arms above my head and yawned. "Fuck, I'm tired. When are we going back to bed?" We'd been running all night for three days straight to get home in time for Christmas, and we'd made it with just a few days to spare. But I was fucking exhausted.

"You can go now if you want," Jase said, rolling his eyes at me. "But I'm getting some proper food in me first."

We'd stopped by our parents' places long enough to grab some clothes and say 'hi' to a few people, but we were all in desperate need of a relaxing warm shower and a hot meal.

Jase grabbed his knife and fork and held them as he waited for our food to arrive.

I groaned and went back to rolling my neck and shoulders, trying in vain to stretch out the muscles that were knotted as shit. "God, I'm sore. Being in shifter mode for too long messes with my back."

"Oh, my God," Fin said, glaring at me. "Would you stop your whining? We're home. We're starving. And Toni will be over with your burger soon. So just shut up. What more do you want?"

"Yeah, home and single. Still," I said, snorting in annoyance. I stared down at the table, going over the menu once again. Nothing had changed in the year we'd been gone. Nothing at all. "When are we leaving again?"

Fin stared at me like I'd grown a second head. "You want to leave again, already?"

I nodded. "Why not? Nothing's changed around here. We're still single and the pack still can't have daughters. I'm not going to sit around here and just wait for insanity." The loneliness of not having a mate got to me more than anything. Sometimes I thought I'd go crazy from a lack of touch—just some basic flesh to flesh affection.

Toni arrived with our food, cutting off my complaints.

"Looks great, thanks Toni," Jase said, grinning up at the girl we'd grown up with, but who'd ended up mating with one of the guys ten years older than us.

"Enjoy," she said with a grin. "It's good to have you guys back."

I didn't say anything, but grabbed my burger with both hands, watching the yellow egg yolk ooze over the greasy bacon and drip onto the fries beneath, absorbing the fatty goodness. I took a big bite, the juiciness of the meat patty, the cheese, and the freshness of the salad making me moan in bliss. *God*, we hadn't had enough good meals lately.

Jase laughed at me while he cut up his steak. "Hungry then?"

"Mmm... hm." I nodded and kept eating, sating a hunger I hadn't realized I'd been ignoring. Another problem with being in wolf form too long: None of us liked to hunt down animals and eat them raw the way normal wild wolves did. But if we didn't eat, by the time we were back in human form, we were absolutely ravenous. Shifting took a toll on our energy.

I ate my huge burger and all the fries, then stared at the pies on the counter. "I think I might go check out dessert."

"Go for it," Fin said, sitting back and rubbing his belly after downing his own burger. "Whatever you order, get me one too!"

I nodded with a grin and headed off to the front counter, inhaling deeply as the sweet smell of cherry pie filled my nostrils. *Mmm. Hell yes.* I grinned at Toni. "Can you bring over three slices of cherry pie with extra cream, please?"

Toni picked up her pad and pen and scrawled a note on it. "Sorry, Ollie. We have peach pie today. That okay?"

I sniffed again, my brow furrowing. "I'm sure I can smell cherries..." I drifted off as the scent grew stronger and stronger.

The bell above the door to the café rang.

I turned around to see who was walking in at the weird time between lunch and dinner and froze.

The three wolf shifters I knew well enough. I'd grown up with Jackson and Billy, and everyone knew the weird warlock-wolf Darren. But what had my heart beating in my throat was the sight of the woman standing with them. Not the brunette, though she was cute. It was the blonde.

Wow. I opened my mouth to call out to them but found myself growling low in my throat instead. *What the hell?* I put my hand up to signal to them.

Then Billy grabbed the blonde by the arm to get her attention and pointed at me.

I saw red. What the hell was he doing touching her? I charged for Billy, dancing around the tables and pushing chairs out of my way. They clattered to the floor in my wake. I heard someone yell out, but I didn't care. Billy had to take his hands off her. *Now.* Nothing was going to stop me getting hold of the guy touching my—

"Whoa, slow down, Ollie." Jackson surged forward, blocking my path. He grabbed me by both arms and pressed hard, stopping me in my tracks.

I growled at him.

He barked back. "Get a hold of yourself."

Jackson was an Alpha while Billy and I were both Betas. And though we didn't give much kudos to the original hierarchy of the pack, my genetics demanded that I listen to Jackson.

I shook myself and growled again, unable to speak though I

wanted to. My teeth had shifted, and the sharp points of my fangs cut into my bottom lip. "I…"

"I know. You're struggling to control your wolf. You can't speak. And you want to kill Billy for touching Tiffany. I know. I can see it written all over your face."

I stared up at him. *How the hell does he know that?*

"Billy, just step away from Tiff for a bit, okay?" Jackson called over his shoulder, not taking his hands off my arms.

Billy took a decent sideways step.

My wolf calmed down instantly. My teeth retracted into my gums, and I could finally speak again. "Thanks."

"I'm not sure this was a good idea," Darren said, sidling up to the blonde that was making my wolf go berserk.

I growled at him.

Behind me, Fin and Jase hurried to join us.

"What's wrong? What's going on? What—" Fin's words were cut off as he too growled.

I glared at him. *What the fuck is wrong with us?*

"We better get outside. Quick," Darren said, tugging on the blonde and the brunette.

The girls followed him out the door without complaint.

I glanced back at my two best friends.

Their eyes were wild, and they looked as out of control as I was feeling. *There better be a good explanation for this.*

Jackson shook me a little. "Oliver. Look at me. Focus."

I stared up at him and clenched my jaw. He was an Alpha. I would listen to him and do as he said.

"You need to hold yourself together for two more minutes. Then you can shift and run until your heart's content, okay? I'll come with you. But do *not* let go of your wolf yet. Got it?"

I nodded as I gritted my teeth.

He glanced over at Fin and Jase. "You two as well. Agreed?"

They grunted their assent, and we stormed out into the open air together.

I inhaled deeply, finding it somehow easier to control the racing of my heart while we were outside, and I could no longer smell just how sweet the blonde was in the open air. Thankfully, I was standing upwind of her, and that gave me enough of a reprieve that I could get a handle on my wolf. "What's this?" I managed to get out between my teeth.

Jackson stood between us three guys and the two girls who were huddled together, staring at us.

Damn, she was beautiful. Long blonde hair, full lips, gorgeous blue eyes...

What I didn't like was the fact that Billy and Darren stood on either side of the girls as though they needed protecting. I could tell they were ready for a fight if it came down to it, and I found myself weighing up the pros and cons of taking them on.

Jackson was an Alpha, and we'd struggle to take him down, but the other two would be easier between the three of us.

A moment later two huge Alphas wandered up to the group. They grabbed the brunette up in their arms and both kissed her.

I glanced over at Fin and Jase. The tide had just turned. We wouldn't win this fight, no matter what we did now. Especially if we had to go up against that one... His name was Elliot. He was bigger than any Alpha I'd ever seen, and there were stories about his temper. They called him an Alpha's *Alpha.*

But as I watched him with the woman who had to be his mate, his care and affection showed a side to him I'd never expected to see. A softer side.

I took a step back, relaxing my stance. *Who are these girls?*

Jackson grinned at us. "Okay, you know what? I'm going to give you the crash course in everything you need to know. We've learned from experience what lies and secrets can do so I'm going give you the easy road. A path I wish I'd been able to take."

"Hurry," Fin said, trembling behind me. He was losing control of his wolf.

I reached out and pulled him back with me a bit. "It's easier if you're further away."

Fin didn't really like being in wolf form when he didn't have to be, so he would find this test harder than most.

Jackson nodded. "Okay. Well, basically, our mates are witches. They have three wolf mates each. Mine, Billy's, and Darren's mate isn't here. She's sick at home. Bella is mated to Elliot, Jonah, and Tommy. And Tiffany over there?" he said, gesturing to the gorgeous blonde. "Is yours."

My mouth dropped open. "No fucking way." I wasn't sharing my mate with anyone else! And there's no way Fate would send me a witch mate. That's not how things worked around here.

Jackson laughed. "*Yes,* way. Get over the fact they're witches, because they're half wolf shifter as well. They're the daughters of the Manterri cousins who went missing over twenty years ago."

"Seriously?" Jase asked.

"Tell them about the love spell," the blonde—Tiffany—called out.

I groaned at the effect her voice had on my inner wolf. I growled as my teeth began to shift once more. *Damn, she is sweet, and sexy, and hot.* More than anything I wanted to grab her, pull her beneath me, and sink my cock into her... I shook my head. *Focus!*

Jackson nodded. "The three girls cast a love spell on Halloween last year, calling for their soul mates. They didn't realize it would bring three wolf shifters for each of them."

Darren moved closer to Jackson. "But it isn't a spell that makes you love them, when you shouldn't. It just called out to us. Fate made us for them, and them for us."

"You. All. Share?" I managed to ask through gritted teeth with difficulty.

"Really?" Fin added.

Elliot laughed, the sound dark and deep. "You get over the jealousy crap." He shrugged. "They're worth it." He snuggled his tiny mate.

something shifted inside my chest.

I looked at Fin and Jase. "You guys feeling the same thing I am?

Seriously?" These two guys were my best friends, my brothers-in-arms, but I'd never shared a woman with them, even on a casual night. I certainly never thought I'd have to share a Fated Mate for the rest of my lives with them.

They frowned at me,

So, I elaborated. "My mate's the blonde."

Fin nodded. "Yep."

"Me too," Jase added.

Tiffany squealed in this gorgeous way.

It made me want to go over and grab her. She sounded excited. Hell, she sounded hot. What sort of noises would she make when I got her into bed? Correction. When *we* got her into bed... I took a step toward her.

Jackson put out a hand and pressed it against my chest. "Ah. No. Trust me when I say you need a minute to process this. The girls will grab your clothes and we'll meet back at..." Jackson glanced at Tiffany.

Our mate whispered something to the brunette.

"Our place," said the brunette. "Let's leave Ruby to rest."

Jackson nodded then turned back to me, his jaw tight. "Okay. Let's go. To be honest, I could use a run too."

I groaned. "But we've been running for three days straight to get home in time for Christmas."

Jackson raised an eyebrow. "Which is probably the *only* reason you haven't wolfed out and lost control already. But seriously, let's go. You two as well." He pointed to Jase and Fin.

Jase tore off his shirt.

Tiffany's eyes bulged, and she licked her lips.

Oh, it was like that, was it? I ripped off my sweater and tossed it to the ground, staring at the woman I'd just been told was my mate. I'd traveled the whole fucking country, and she'd been right here all along? Just waiting for us to find her? A witch? A gorgeous half shifter? *Who I have to share with my two best friends.*

"Fucking hell," I said, then as I caught her eye, I saluted her and grinned the best I could manage. "See you soon." I let go of my humanity and shifted. I didn't like being in my wolf body as much as my human form, but it was an easy enough transition.

Jackson, Fin, and Jase shifted as well.

I took a moment to stare at my mate, or the woman Jackson had declared was mine at least. But it had to be true. *What other reason can there be for how I feel?* I wanted to kiss her, hold her, tuck her into my body, and keep her safe for all of time. And my wolf felt the same way. Every part of me acknowledged that she was the woman I'd been desperately searching for.

Jase nudged me with his head and with one last look at Tiffany's smiling, beautiful face, we took off, through the town, around several new buildings I'd never seen before, and dashed off into the forest.

Jackson took us the long way around the pack, running us through the woods and further than we'd normally go. We ran all the way to the witches' church and circled back home to the pack again.

Home. A place I'd thought was where dreams went to die. A place I'd initially refused to return to when Jase and Fin had wanted to, until my mom had called and begged for us to visit for Christmas.

But I could admit it now. This place, this pack, was where my heart truly lay. I'd just been so disappointed with how my life had turned out —so fucking lonely— that I'd run away from everything I'd ever known in an attempt to change it.

Now things were different. For the first time in forever, as we ran home, my wolf howled with happiness. After months, no, *years* of searching, our mate had found us. Finally.

Now we just had to sort out where we were going to live, and who she was going to sleep with. I'd bunked with Fin and Jase for way too many months, and I had no intention of sharing my mate with them. And I was damn sure they felt the exact same way about me.

CHAPTER 4

TIFFANY

"Oh, my God, oh, my God, *oh, my God!*" I couldn't help the ridiculous words and nonsensical squealing that spilled out of me as the men shifted and ran away. *God, they were beautiful.* All three of them. And they were mine! I couldn't believe it. I slammed both hands over my mouth in an attempt to mute myself.

Bella laughed at me. "I knew they'd come for you. You just had to wait a little longer."

I deserved the 'I told you so' and I honestly didn't even care. I jumped at my best friend, sweeping her up into an epic hug and squeezing her tight. I never wanted to let go of these incredible feelings coursing through my veins. I literally shook with excitement, so happy I wanted to cry.

"They're good guys," Billy said from behind me. "Jackson and I grew up with them. They'll look after you, Tiff."

I drew back to stare at him, realizing I should probably ask him some questions—get some basic information on my three brand new mates. "Who are they? What are their names? What do they do?"

Before Billy could answer, Elliot interrupted. "And not that I mind, of course, but how come everyone's coming back to our place? We haven't built the extension yet. It's going to get super crowded real fast."

I hadn't thought about that. Bella's house was tiny, made for two bachelors who'd never planned on finding their mates. Now, there were four of them living there, and adding us into the equation was going to make things squeezy.

"You know, I've been thinking. Rather than extending, it might be easier to just buy that big place we were looking at last week," Tommy said. "Especially if Bella's going to have Tiff and Ruby around all the time. They each come in packs of four..."

I laughed, almost hysterically. *I* was included now, no longer left behind like an afterthought.

Then Bella answered Elliot's question, sobering us all. "Well, uh, Ruby's in some sort of sleep at the moment. Our moms are there looking after her, so I didn't really think it was a good idea to go back to Jackson's place and disturb everyone."

Elliot's smile dropped. "Shit. I had no idea, Bell. What's wrong with her? Do they know?"

"Is it the baby?" Tommy asked.

"Yeah, it is," Bella said quietly, almost reluctantly. "I'll explain as we walk. Grab some of the clothes with me Tiff, then let's go," Bella said, tugging on my arm.

I scooped up two pairs of jeans and a hoodie from the ground where the guys had left their clothes after they'd shifted. Bella grabbed the rest, and we walked away from Milly's and toward Bella's current accommodation.

The men and Bella discussed Ruby's condition.

I managed to wrangle Billy away from the group. "Hey, what can you tell me about my mates?" I asked.

Billy grinned at me. "The one who was doing most of the talking? That's Oliver, but everyone calls him Ollie. He's a grumpy bastard like me, but he's cool."

A guy like Billy? *Yeah*, I could totally cope with that.

"The other two are Fin and Jason. All three of them are Betas, so hopefully you won't need to deal with the overly jealous Alpha bullshit."

"Hey," Jackson called from behind us.

Billy just shrugged off his Alpha's playful protest before addressing me once more. "They were the only guys to leave the pack and look for their mate in other states. Even though everyone here is miserable, they actually did something about it. So, they've always been pretty determined to find you."

I bit my lip. That sounded like a dream. Men who wanted me... and only me. Men who'd traveled the whole country in their efforts to find me. "Thanks, Billy." *I needed that.*

We arrived at Bella's house which was a neat and tidy two-bedroom, two story house. It was much smaller than Ruby's place, but they obviously had plans to buy something bigger to accommodate them all as they were discussing. Especially, now that they were a family of four, and not two.

Billy began to back away. "I think I'll get going back to the house."

Darren went with him. "Me too. I want to check in on Ruby."

"Thanks guys," I said, rearranging the clothes I held to grip them tighter against my chest. Damn they smelled good. "Thanks for everything. I really appreciate you introducing us and everything. I'll message my mom later and see if the Coven needs our help trying to find a cure for all this."

We'd been doing research, and spells, trying to find the source of the curse so we could unhook it from ourselves. But with Ruby's sudden illness, and the fact she was carrying the only hope for future generations, finding a solution would become everyone's number one priority.

"You need to concentrate on your mates," Bella said, turning toward me and giving me a pointed stare. "If that's the key, us all needing to find love with the wolves; once you're mated, the curse might break."

I inhaled sharply at the thought of finally mating—of losing my virginity—and my chest tightened with anxiety. "It's definitely worth a shot," I admitted. I didn't really like the idea of ignoring Ruby's current plight to focus on my mates, but considering they were all I'd ever wanted, hopefully it would all come easily between us, and we'd soon have some kind of solution or answer. Just as Bella suggested. Which meant I'd be helping Ruby as well! *Not to mention our fathers.*

"We need to get back to work too," Elliot said, glancing at Tommy. "Or do you think one of us should stay here, you know, just in case."

Tommy nodded. "I'll stay, it's cool. Jackson will probably want to get back to Ruby when he returns. Someone should supervise the Betas."

He was probably right. If Jackson, Tommy, and Elliot were all gone, that only left Bella, me, and three men that I'd just met half an hour ago.

Elliot pecked Bella on the lips. "I'll only be a few hours, beautiful, but call if you need me to come home earlier."

Bella nodded and cupped her mate's face in a sweet caress that made my heart ache. "Thanks, Elliot."

He gave me a quick smile and bounded away.

"Come inside," Bella said, taking my hand and dragging me into the house.

When we stepped over the threshold, I glanced around. "Where do you guys all sleep? In one bedroom, like Ruby does?"

Bella's face turned a bright shade of crimson red.

I laughed. "Oh, come on, Bell. Don't be embarrassed." I put the guys' clothes down on the nearby couch.

Bella did the same with the articles she'd carried.

Tommy chuckled, grabbing sodas from the fridge, and tossed us each one. "Yeah. We all sleep in Elliot's room at the moment. It's on this floor, so easy access to the kitchen and he has the biggest bed. But if we get the new house that Elliot and I looked at last week, we'll be able to have two king beds in the one room and put them together. The master room is massive on that one."

"Which house is this?" Bella asked.

"The one near Jackson's," Tommy said casually. "One of the Elders built it for his son and grandkids, but they decided they couldn't afford the loan… And, anyway, not our business. But it's *big*. And it'll suit us in the future."

Tommy and Bella shared a pointed look.

I raised my eyebrows. "Don't tell me you're pregnant, already, too?"

"Oh, God no." Bella laughed, waving a hand as though dismissing my words. "But we do want kids. One day."

"Definitely," Tommy said with a broad grin. "As many as Bella will agree to."

Bella rolled her eyes. "I know, I know. Just let me finish college first," she added playfully.

I sighed and sank onto the couch, basking in their happiness. This morning I was so insanely jealous of what my friends had found that I would have curled into a ball and died if I'd had to listen to a sweet conversation like this again. But now that I knew my men had finally found me, I could relax and be at home around these people. *My people.* I truly, finally belonged and would be getting my happily ever after! "So, how many years have you got to go again, Bell? One?" I asked.

"Yeah, but that's not important at the moment. Tell me how you're feeling! Relieved that the love spell worked to bring your triad to you?"

I laughed. "A triad… Such a strange concept still."

Bella snorted. "Yeah, I know. When Ruby got three mates, my only thought was, *'God no, I could never do that'.*"

"What changed?" I probed curiously.

She shrugged. "Well, when you're in it, feeling it rather than just looking in from the outside, it feels right. Your perspective changes and you realize that it's natural, and normal, and perfect." She exchanged a glance with Tommy that made my insides twist and turn.

"I hope my triad will be as happy with me, as you guys obviously are, together," I said.

Tommy grinned and saluted me by lifting his can of soda. "They will be. That's the magic of Fated Mates. Even if there's crap at the start, jealousy and fights, you already know you're destined to be together and it makes you keep pushing forward, no matter what hurdles get in your way."

Bella sat on the couch and curled her legs up under her. "That's true. I struggled to believe it myself at the start. I thought that it would be better to let Elliot go, and just be with Jonah and Tommy. It seemed so much easier to be with them."

"Naw, thanks babe," Tommy said with a lop-sided grin.

I hadn't heard about this. "You were really going to let Elliot go?"

I stared at her; partly sure she'd gone crazy. Elliot was *hot*, with a capital H. Like crazy muscly, with a gorgeous face and a protective streak a mile wide. *What wasn't to like?*

Bella bit her lip and pulled a huge gray pillow onto her lap, hugging it tight to herself like a makeshift plush shield. "Yeah, well, at the time, I figured he was part of the punishment for using the love spell. The debt of pain I was meant to pay. I mean, I wanted him. I wanted him so much it hurt. But we're so different. I never thought we could make a relationship work."

I swallowed hard. *Shit!* "The payment... I'd totally forgotten about that part." Using the love spell had its consequences. Payment for services rendered. If the spell worked, it took something from you in return. I didn't want to lose my magic like Ruby had, or any of my mates like Bella almost had.

Bella shrugged. "We're here for you. No matter what. I'm sure everything's going to be okay."

I pulled my hair out of its high ponytail and ran my hands through the tangles. "Yeah, I suppose. *If* we can work out a way to break the curse."

Bella glanced out the door. "Speaking of which, I really should go visit my dad. It's been a few days since I last popped in."

I moved further along the couch and arranged myself in the corner of the chaise. "It's hard when they can't talk back, isn't it? But I still like hanging out with them."

She nodded, her eyes lighting up. "Yeah, me too."

"Do you think we'll ever get them back as, you know, humans?" I asked. Yesterday, it was my greatest wish, outside of finding my mates.

Bella inhaled slowly, then sighed. "I really hope so."

I slipped off my shoes and tucked my legs up under myself so I could cuddle into the couch the way Bella was. "Do you think they'll get back together, if we manage to get the dads back to their human forms?"

"Who?" Bella asked.

I grinned. "Our moms and dads, of course. All of them are still single. So, do you think they'll all just, you know, pick up where they left off twenty-three years ago?"

My mom had had so little time with my dad. One single night, after only a short time of dating. It seemed incredibly unfair.

Bella frowned, worry lines creasing her forehead. "I honestly don't know."

"If they're Fated Mates, they'll have no choice," Tommy said, his deep voice booming across the room. "They'll see each other again once the guys are in human form, and that'll be it. They'll have to be together. The fact that none of your moms remarried indicates they probably felt the bond."

"None of them have even tried dating," I said, feeling like that was a point that should be made. "I even encouraged my mom to date. When I was little, I'd point out the warlocks in the Coven who'd stare at her, or even humans in town I thought were nice. But she was never interested in any of them."

Bella shook her head. "My mom, either."

Tommy grunted. "Sounds like Fated Mates to me."

I opened my mouth to ask more questions about wolves and their mates, But the thud of loud footfalls landing on the porch sounded. I jumped to my feet, my heart thundering in my chest. They were here!

The front door burst open and four very naked men walked in. I didn't so much as glance at Jackson, but I couldn't help but stare at my three guys.

God, they are so beautiful. Lean. Muscled. Hard. Perfect.

"Do you guys mind if I head home? I want to go see Ruby." Jackson grabbed his jeans and pulled them on.

"Of course not. Go," I said.

"Thanks," he said before he scooped up his hoodie and headed for the door.

"I'll hang around," Tommy answered. "But let us know if Ruby wakes up."

Jackson saluted and headed out the door.

Once he was gone, I swallowed hard, unable to speak as I stared my men. My throat ached, and my belly was tight. *Oh, my God. So many men.* How was I ever going to handle all of... that?

The three guys stared at me with varying degrees of curiosity and sexual heat.

My face flamed with the blush of embarrassment and a hint of lust.

"Here you go, guys," Bella said, scooping up their clothes we'd carried home and dumping them in the middle of the room. "Throw some clothes on."

They nodded and began to re-dress.

I couldn't drag my eyes away from them and their incredible bodies, so strong and rippled with muscles. I didn't even bother trying to hide it. *They were mine, weren't they?* Three gray wolves, and me... their blonde witch.

CHAPTER 5

JASE

I clenched my jaw, my wolf flaring hard inside of me. I wanted to grab her and fuck her. I couldn't believe how strong the desire was. I normally prided myself on being pretty cool. Fun. Easy. But at this moment? Damn, I wanted my mate naked and under me.

I forced myself to pull on my jeans and sweater over my overheated body, my skin tingling and itchy with the need for a long shower. I tore my gaze from her gorgeous face and stared at Tommy. "Hey, man. I know it's early but..."

"You want a beer? Yeah. Of course." Tommy pulled a six pack from the fridge. "I know. I've needed a few of these myself since finding my mate." He handed me a bottle, then offered them to Ollie and Fin.

They took one each.

We weren't usually big drinkers, but today was a celebration day.

I think.

Fin glanced at me, and we both looked at Tiffany.

Where the hell do we go from here?

Fin walked over to the couch; his hand extended in greeting. "We weren't technically introduced earlier. I'm Fin."

Tiffany stood up off the couch, wobbling.

I rushed forward instinctively, grabbing onto her arms to support her. "Are you okay?" A shot of silver lightning pierced my nerves, pleasure shivering through my arm as we touched. "Holy shit…" I staggered sideways.

She grabbed for me, momentary panic in her eyes.

Another bolt of pleasure passed through me, and although I managed to stifle the moan—she didn't.

The groan that came from her throat sounded like she was aching for me just as much as I ached for her. It moved through me like a prayer, fulfilling every wish I'd ever had for myself.

I pulled her with me onto the couch.

"What was that?" Fin asked, frowning suspiciously at me.

I swallowed hard. I didn't really want to tell him, but if we were meant to be co-mates, I needed to man up and share. "Touch her, man. You'll feel it, I think."

Tiffany's eyes went wide.

I smiled reassuringly at her. "Go on. Try it."

"Okay." Tiffany put out her hand to Fin.

He gripped it and pulled her to her feet.

They both shivered as though someone had walked over their graves, as the saying went, though it was the complete opposite in this case. We'd just met our future. Our lives were only just beginning.

"Whoa," Fin said.

I turned around to call out to Mr. Grumpy Ass. "Hey, Ollie. Come over here."

Ollie strolled over with a grimace. "I'm Oliver."

She bowed her head sweetly. "I'm Tiffany."

She held out her delicate hand, her arm shaking. From apprehension, or nerves, I wasn't sure.

Ollie reached out and grabbed her hand, a moan escaping his lips as his eyes went wide.

Tiffany began to faint and all three of us jumped to grab her. We all connected, touching her at once, and the feeling was positively electric. Like touching a live wire, but in a good way.

I gasped.

We all panted as one but didn't move away, none of us willing to let her go.

She struggled to breathe as well, but turned to me, her blue eyes wide, her pupils huge and dilated with arousal. "And you're...?"

"Jase," I said. "Well, it's Jason, but I prefer Jase."

She wet her lips by sneaking out her tongue and licking them.

The move made me ache hard to kiss her. "So, what's next?" I asked, trying not to focus on how badly I wanted her. We had to take this slow. We couldn't rush and spook our Fated Mate.

Her beautiful lips lifted up into a grin. "Um, we move into a house and live happily ever after?"

And that was all it took. The beautiful atmosphere in the room broke as if Tiffany had dropped a crystal vase on the tiles beneath her feet.

All three of us stepped away.

Tiffany nearly collapsed.

The brunette rushed over to grab Tiffany's hand. "Are you okay? What was that all about?"

I frowned at the girl, who glared at us. "Um, and you're...?"

"I'm Bella," she said, straightening her spine but narrowing her eyes at me. "I'm mated to Elliot, Tommy, and Jonah."

"Jonah?" Fin asked. "Billy's little brother. He's a nice kid."

Bella pressed her lips together. "We're the same age. How old are you?"

From the kitchen, Tommy watched, shaking his head and grinning.

"Finding this amusing, huh?" I called out to him.

"Oh yeah," he said, joining us in the living room. "I was standing in your shoes a month ago, and I don't envy you at all. Speaking of which, I think I'm going to take my mate for a walk and show her the house we want to buy for her. Something nice and big." He grabbed Bella's hand.

"But…" she started to say.

"I think Tiff and the guys need a few minutes alone to talk. We won't be long. Twenty minutes tops." He glanced at Tiffany. "If that's okay with you?"

She nodded. "I'm pretty good at offensive spells. If any of them piss me off…" She raised her eyebrows and stared at each of us in turn. "They'll find out what a witch can do."

I took a step back and put up my hands. "We won't hurt you. I promise. Never." I'd never laid a finger on a woman, and as far as I knew, neither had Fin or Ollie.

"I think we should stay," Bella said, glancing at each of us as though she didn't approve of us. At all.

"Come on, sweetheart." Tommy dragged his reluctant mate from the room and closed the door behind them.

The room went quiet. Unnervingly so.

Tiffany slid onto the couch and indicated to the room. "Have a seat and explain to me what the hell just happened."

I grabbed a chair from the dining table, turned it around, and plonked myself down onto it.

Fin and Ollie found a spot on the large couch but didn't go anywhere near our new mate.

She'd really dumped a bucket of cold water on us with that comment about expecting a happily ever after. And a house. Did she want a baby by tomorrow, too? Although getting her pregnant sure would be fun, I wasn't sure I wanted kids so soon.

"Which part?" I asked, making sure I knew what she was talking about before I put my foot in it.

She rolled her eyes and sighed dramatically.

I blinked. Had she really just done that? I looked at the other guys, who were just as surprised as me.

"The part where we were all connected and hot, and I said something about a happily ever after and you all recoiled like typical human guys. What's wrong? Are you all afraid of commitment or something?"

My mouth gaped open. "Afraid of commitment? Us? We've just spent the last year traveling from state to state, looking for our mates."

Tiffany raised an eyebrow. "And how did you test these women to find out if they were your mates, exactly?"

"Oh, well…" I glanced at the floor, then over at the guys, hoping they'd take one for the team.

"So, you didn't just hold their hand, and test if there was a connection or not?" she pressed.

I met her gaze. She couldn't possibly think we'd gone all this time without a woman in our bed? What sort of men did she take us for? I forced out a laugh. "You don't need to lecture us. We all have a past. It's not like you're a virgin…"

"Yes, I am," she said, lifting her head and straightening her spine like she was affronted.

My mouth dropped open. "Are you serious?" I asked. "But you'd have to be, what, twenty-two, twenty-three?" That was, if my fast calculations about when the Manterri cousins went missing were right.

"I turned twenty-two on Halloween a few months ago. What's your point?" she asked, glaring at me.

"That you can't be a virgin," Ollie burst out "You're too fucking hot!"

Tiffany's cheeks went a bright shade of pink. "Well, while I appreciate the backhanded compliment, I have to inform you that no-one's wanted me before." She stood up and walked to the door. "And since you three seem to think I'm a liar, I think I'll join the rest of the guys and go hang out at Jackson's."

"No!" I said, jumping to my feet. "I'm sorry… I mean, we didn't mean to say you were lying. Of course, you wouldn't lie about something like that. But I've never had a…" I glanced at the other two guys.

They shook their heads.

"We've," I corrected myself, "never had a virgin."

Tiffany sniffed and wiped away the tears I hadn't even seen her cry. "Well, you still haven't, but I've been waiting for you. *Properly*. I haven't been fucking my way around the country, pretending I was looking for the right guy. So, excuse me while I check on my friend. At least her mates didn't run a mile when they found out she waited for them!" She flicked her gorgeous blonde hair over her shoulder, walked through the door, and slammed it shut on her way out.

I stared at the closed door, speechless. "Did that really just happen?" None of this made any sense. How had we gone from practically panting for her, to losing her in the next breath?

Ollie paced the room, cussing under his breath.

I sat down on the dining table chair and leaned back. "I don't get it." I shook my head. "Women."

"Well, it's her fault we freaked out, a bit," Ollie said, staring at me like I needed to agree with him. "We haven't even gotten to kiss her yet, and she's already talking about us buying her a house. What sort of chick does that?"

Fin huffed out a laugh. "*All* of them."

"Yeah, because they want the guy to pay for everything," I said.

We all chuckled, but beneath the laughter I could hear the thread of tension.

For guys of almost thirty, we didn't have anything to offer her. The other two guys knew it, and I knew it. When we'd been younger, we'd spent most of the money we made on food and booze and going out. There had been no reason to save for a rainy day—especially when there was no sign of a mate on the horizon.

Then last year when we'd decided to leave the pack, the little we'd saved had gone into travel expenses. We'd had to pick up some casual work along the way to pay our way as well, but we virtually had nothing left.

Fin sighed. "She's going to be disappointed when she realizes we can buy her sweet diddly-squat. I was planning on just crashing with my parents for a few days, before we headed off again."

"But if she's the one for us, we're staying, right?" I asked the others. "I mean, the whole point of traveling around was to look for our mates, and now that we've found her..."

"And we have to share her," Ollie said with a soft growl. "How do you guys feel about that?"

Silence descended over us. We were all Betas. None of us had a wide, arrogant Alpha streak. But none of us had prepared for this eventuality either.

"Well... I mean, it's not a preference," I said.

"God, no," Ollie said.

"I agree," Fin said. "But I don't care enough to walk away or anything. I mean, I'm not going to leave again to see if I can find another mate somewhere else. Do either of you want to try that after what we just felt?"

I crossed my arms over my chest and shook my head. "Not me. I've had enough of the loneliness."

A wolf shifter was a pack animal. A family man. Not having a mate, or the prospect of children, was what had driven us to leave our pack behind in the first place.

Tiffany was ours—mine—and despite this hiccup I wasn't leaving without her.

"Unless she wants to come with us? I mean, if you guys want to travel more, I'd be up for that. But she'd need to come along too."

Ollie scowled, still walking around the tidy little lounge room. "That's not likely. She'll have roots here. A family. Plus, you heard what she said. She wants a house. A big expensive one probably, like Tommy was talking about buying his mate."

Fin shrugged. "Looks like we've got to get jobs again then to support her."

"Yeah, and work out where we're going to sleep while we try to woo our mate back," I added, hating the idea that we'd pissed her off so royally already. "I'm not sure about you, but the shock has kind of worn off, now. And I'm starting to like the idea that she hasn't been with anyone else."

I more than liked it, truth be told. I fucking *loved* the idea that her pussy was waiting for me to be the one to taste it for the first time.

Ollie frowned.

But Fin laughed at me. "Yeah. It's hot."

"We've just got to convince her to give us another shot, I suppose." Worry settled in my chest, because the longer I sat here thinking about it, the more I realized we'd probably stuffed up a pretty critical time in the dating program. *Shit.*

CHAPTER 6

FIN

I slapped myself in the head. *Oh, my God.* Jase could be so dense! We needed help. That was for God damn sure. I got to my feet and looked straight at Bella. "Um, we scared her off."

Bella frowned.

Tommy just laughed and headed for the kitchen.

He opened the fridge. "You guys hungry?"

I shook my head. "We ate at Milly's just before you arrived."

Tommy ignored my statement and started rummaging through his huge silver fridge.

Bella crossed her arms over her chest. "What did you do?"

Ollie threw his hands up in the air. "We didn't do… anything!"

She raised an eyebrow and gave me a reproachful look. "Fin?"

"Um, it's kind of hard to explain." I ran a hand through my hair that had grown to my shoulders. It needed a good cut, and I needed a long shower—two things that may have also contributed to our mate running for the damn hills.

"I'm not dumb, so about you try me?" Bella said.

There was an answering chuckle from the kitchen. The sound of the microwave could be heard a moment later, before the smell of fragrant lamb curry filled the room.

"What are you laughing at?" I asked Tommy, putting off the inevitable conversation with Bella a little longer.

He laughed louder. "You guys. If you knew how good it is to finally have a mate to love, you'd be chasing Tiffany down and begging forgiveness for whatever stupid thing you did."

My stomach tightened. A warning. We needed to listen to this guy.

I sighed and looked at Bella. "Tiffany said she was going to head over to Ruby's house. Could you show us the way?"

"Yeah, it's not far," Bella said, reaching for a purple sweater I hadn't noticed lying on the back of the sofa.

Outside it was getting darker and colder, not that we cared. As wolf shifters we never felt the cold, but as a witch, Bella wasn't so lucky. And from the way she shivered before wrapping the sweater around her shoulders and buttoning it up, she obviously felt it.

I made a mental note. *Tiffany's going to feel the cold in the future. So, no more sleeping outside or leaving all the windows open in winter.*

"You're not going to run after her, are you?" Ollie asked me, looking shocked.

I rounded on him. "Yeah, of course I am. Aren't you coming?"

Of the three of us, Ollie was the most cantankerous. A right pain in the ass most of the time. But he was as loyal and fierce as the day was long, so we put up with the other shit.

Ollie's jaw set.

I knew his answer. "Fine," I said, before I turned to Jase. "How about you? You coming?"

Jase looked between Ollie and me and frowned. "I'm not rapt about sharing a mate, but I'm damn sick of running all over the state looking for her. So, if Tiffany is the one for us, I'm in, no matter what I have to do." He stood up from his spot on the couch.

I assumed that meant he'd suck it up and get to work if we needed to buy a house for our new mate. He *did* say 'no matter what' after all. "Then let's go." I turned to Bella. "Lead the way."

Fin and I followed Bella out of the house and headed down the street. We didn't talk for a block or two, but soon Bella was at us again.

"Tiffany's one of the easiest people to get along with on the planet," Bella said. "She's super easygoing and doesn't take too much seriously, which is usually a plus. I don't get what you guys could have done to upset her enough that she would actually get up and leave."

I turned to Jase. "Um…"

Jase shrugged. "It's hard to explain, but we'll sort it out. We've probably spent too long on the road. We're a bit rusty on the talking to sensitive women front."

"Sensitive women?" Bella repeated, her voice rising higher as though she was mocking us.

"And the last thing we expected her to be, was a virgin. That was a bit of a shock too," he continued.

Bella stopped in her tracks.

Jase and I had to turn back around to look at her.

She held up both of her hands, her face twisting with anger. "Hang on a second. I'm sorry, but am I getting this right? She told you she was a virgin, and you guys… you possessive, protective, *stupid* wolf shifters… didn't want her to be? You thought it was, what, a bad thing that she saved herself for her soul mate?"

I glanced at Jase. "Well, when you put it like that…"

"You guys sound like fucking assholes!" Bella finished for me, crossing her arms over her chest.

I tilted my head and stared at her. "You know, I think I underestimated you."

She rolled her eyes, but the start of a smile played at the edges of her lips. "I may be a bookworm, and a bit of a wallflower, but I have three mates, two of whom are Alphas. So yeah, I'm not as quiet, or as weak as I look."

I nodded, grimacing in agreement. "I'm starting to get that." The very last thing we should do was underestimate our own mate, either.

"And Tiffany's not as tough as she looks," Bella said. "Everyone thinks because Tiff's the pretty one, that she's dumb, and slutty, and super confident or something. But she's got weaknesses and soft spots. And yes, she's still a virgin. We *all* swore to each other we'd wait for the right guy. Or in this case, *guys.* Why do you three have such a big problem with that?"

She swallowed and went a little red in the cheeks. "Elliot *loved* that about me—that I'd never been with anyone else, and never would be."

I smiled at her, loving the honesty and vulnerability in her eyes. She was sharing something special about herself so that we didn't screw this up.

"You're right. Of course, you're right. It was just... unexpected."

She cocked an eyebrow at me. "Would you have preferred her to have a list a mile long? Maybe she should try out a few of your pack mates? After all, there's a couple of dozen single guys just waiting for a woman to walk into their lives around here." She gestured to the rows of houses along the street.

A growl rolled through my chest, and

A similar noise came from Jase's throat.

I looked at Jase, surprised by his reaction. He'd always gone for the easy chick. He was too relaxed to work hard in any sort of relationship, especially a one-night stand. Yet he was looking as angry as I felt about Bella making such a suggestion.

When I glanced back at the little witch, she was grinning triumphantly. "*Exactly, you idiots!* You could barely stand it when Billy touched her arm. There's no way you could deal if she even entertained the idea of being with other men. So, next time the topic comes up, keep your bullshit opinions to yourselves." She turned and flicked her long dark hair over her shoulder and marched past us and down the street.

I couldn't help but chuckle as I stared after her. "Where have these sorts of women been all our lives?"

Growing up in a pack that hadn't birthed daughters in a whole generation meant that we'd never dated a lot. By the time we'd reached maturity, there hadn't been a girl born in ten years, and the scrabble for a mate became the obsession of most of the eligible males in our pack.

Jase, Ollie, and I hadn't been old enough to realize just how important it had been to grab whatever available girls there were. And by the time we did, all the good ones had been mated and snaffled up.

So, we'd had to indulge ourselves where we could, finding casual sex with random wolf shifter females from other packs. It had been the best way to deal with our growing sex drives. But we'd never met a girl like this. Strong. Defiant. Loyal to a fault. It was scintillating.

"It's probably because she's a witch," Jase mused. "Bet she's powerful too."

"Too right I am," Bella threw over her shoulder.

I laughed in surprise and amusement, then joined Jase in running to catch up with her.

We walked another couple of blocks together, then came across a massive two-story newly built house.

"Jackson lives here?" I asked, staring up at the monstrosity before us.

Jackson was only a year or two older than us. How did he have the money to afford something like this?

Bella nodded, heading for the side gate. "I'm going to go see my dad for a bit. You two go to the front door and ask Tiff to go for a walk or something. I won't be long. And don't screw this up!" Then Bella disappeared from sight.

I glanced at Jase. "Did she just say she was going into the back yard to talk to her dad? Isn't her dad one of the Manterri cousins?"

Jase shrugged. "I don't know and don't care at this point. Let's just go get Tiffany."

I smiled as we walked up the front steps of the massive house and knocked on the door.

We'd found my mate. *Our* mate. The one we'd been searching for all these years, and we'd finally found her. That was what I needed to focus on. What *we* needed to focus on. Nothing else mattered.

The door opened and an older woman with bright blue eyes opened the door. "Can I help you?" she asked.

"Yeah. We're looking for Tiffany. Is she here?" Jase asked.

I cringed. He sounded like a petulant teenager, not a thirty-year-old man.

The woman narrowed her eyes. "Yes, she is. Who can I say is calling?"

"Um…" Jase stammered under the weight of the woman's protective glare.

I cleared my throat. "I'm sorry. My name is Fin, and this is Jase. She'll know who we are, if you wouldn't mind asking her to come to the door? We'd really appreciate it."

The woman turned to look at me, her gaze flicking up and down my disheveled sweater and jeans. From the way her lip lifted in a slight sneer, it was obvious she found me lacking. She nodded once and closed the door in our faces.

"Do you think that could be Tiffany's mom?" Jase asked.

I tugged on my sweater, wishing I'd had the forethought to go home, have a shower, and get changed. "Yeah, she could be." The blue eyes had been the same.

"Great. Just great," Jase muttered.

"Yeah, we probably didn't make the best first impression."

"Do you think we should go get changed, or something? I mean…" Jase pulled at his hooded sweater. "I didn't think we'd meet our future mate at Milly's today, or I would have had a shave, or something." He ran his hand over his bristled chin and grimaced.

The front door opened, and our blonde mate stood in the doorway, her hair softly floating around her shoulders. Her eyes were red-rimmed.

"Hey, are you okay?" I asked, impulsively reaching out for her.

She shrugged off my hand. "I'm fine. What do you two want?"

"Ah…" I began. We hadn't really thought about what we were going to say when we got here. "We wanted to come over and apologize for our reactions earlier. I think we've been so used to traveling, and being in wolf form, we've lost half our good manners." I ran my hand through my hair and stared at the ground, realizing that it was actually true.

Jase cleared his throat. "Can we maybe take you out for dinner? Or do you want to do something tonight?"

She lifted her chin in a stubborn move that Ollie used all the time. "Where's Oliver?"

Jase chuckled. "You sound like his mom. No-one calls him Oliver except her."

Tiffany flicked her icy glare at Jase and he stopped laughing.

"Sorry," he muttered, put in his place.

Tiffany looked back at me. "I've seen my friends go through a lot of shit with their mates, so here's *my* deal, okay? I've been waiting for you guys for years... literally years... but I'm not going to be angry if one of you wants to jump ship. One woman sharing three guys isn't every-one's bag. I get that. So, I'll meet you at the burger place in town, at seven. It's called Sam's Burgers. Let Ollie know, okay?"

I stared at her, her conviction laden words at odds with her tear-streaked cheeks. "Um, tell Ollie what, exactly?"

"That you've all got one chance. I'm more than ready for my happily ever after. If you guys aren't, well, then, I suppose I'll be eating burgers by myself tonight." She went to close the door,

I put out a hand, pushing against the wood to stop her slamming the door in our faces. "You said Sam's Burgers?"

She nodded once, her mouth pulled tight, and her cheeks pinched. "That's right. In town." With that, she managed to push the door shut in our stupefied faces.

I turned to Jase. "Do you think Ollie can pull himself together in a few hours?"

Jase shook his head. "Nope. Never has before."

I inhaled deeply. This was going to get messy, fast. *Damn it.* If Tiffany and Ollie were as stubborn as each other, we would be in for a long fight. I patted Jase on the back and jogged down the stairs. "Come on. We've got the date of a lifetime to get ready for."

CHAPTER 7

TIFFANY

I moved aside the sheer white curtains on Ruby's front windows and stared at two of my three mates as they jogged off to God-knew-where. Hopefully home to get ready for burgers with me in three hours. But who knew? Life was full of surprises.

"Who were they?" My mom asked from behind me.

I jumped and turned to look at her, momentarily startled. "I think they're my Fated Mates."

Mom's eyes were worried and shadowed as she stared right back at me. "You *think*?"

"I mean, I know. Well..." I shook my head and laughed. I'd never been able to talk to my mom about boys at the best of times. You'd think it would be easier as you got older, but it still wasn't. I shook myself and looked Mom square in the eye. "Their names are Oliver, Jason, and Fin. And yes, they're all my soul mates, Mom. Just like Ruby, and Bella, I have three too."

"Where's the third one?" Mom asked, biting her lip.

I frowned. "He's my problem one."

There was a heavy beat of silence as Mom absorbed my words. Then her lips kicked up at the sides unexpectedly.

"I never told you this, but your dad didn't want to be with me when we first met."

I frowned. She'd never really told me anything about my father, but I hadn't expected that. "What do you mean?"

"I mean..." she turned and glanced toward the kitchen, where I assumed my father in wolf form would be lounging outside the back door on the porch. "He saw that I was a witch and wanted to run in the opposite direction."

"But you told me that you two were only together once," I reminded her.

Mom nodded. "We were. But by that point we'd known each other for almost a year, and it took him that long to get up the courage to follow his instincts and come to me."

"He fought the bond?" I asked, frowning. "Aren't you two Fated Mates?"

Mom sighed. "I'm not sure if we were or not, but I know I wanted him. More than anything. I hated the fact he didn't feel the same way."

"He probably did," I said, defending my dad on instinct. "But sometimes we let other shit get into our heads. Especially when it comes to the whole witches versus wolves thing."

My mom smiled at me. "That's true. So, my point being... don't be too harsh on your third, okay? You should appreciate that, more than anyone. Just because you want something to happen now, and be perfect, doesn't mean it will always work out like that. Unless you've forgotten about Miles?" Mom raised her eyebrows at me.

A flood of shame washed over me, and I looked away, horrified she'd brought up such a thing. I still couldn't believe I'd told her what had happened that night. "Mom. He has nothing to do with *now*."

"Of course, he does," Mom said, and walked over to take my chin in her hand.

I glared at her. "That's not fair."

"It is," Mom said, smiling fondly, despite the daggers I threw at her. "Miles made you feel unloved, unworthy, and undesirable. But you will be *all* of those things to your mates, and so much more. You just need to give them a little time to come up to standard. Guys aren't perfect you know, but then, neither are we." She turned and walked away.

I frowned after her. "What do you mean, 'to standard'?"

She raised an eyebrow at me. "You've had two months to wrap your head around the fact that your mates were probably going to be wolf shifters, and that there would probably be three of them—because you watched it happen with Ruby and Bella, right?"

I nodded, crossing my arms under my breasts. "Yeah, so?"

She chuckled. "These three guys came home for Christmas, according to Bella. They expected to have some food, see their parents, and head off into the wild blue yonder again. They had no idea they were coming home to their Fated Mate, who they now have to share, and who has been raised a full witch."

She stared at me long and hard and said the words she'd said to make me behave ever since I was a kid: "Come on, Tiffany. Be fair." She turned and left the room.

My mouth dropped open. "Be fair? Me! They're the ones that... that..." Don't want me as their mate. Who can't handle the fact they have to share me. And yet I wanted them! *All* of them! I staggered over to the nearby loveseat against the wall and fell onto it, staring around Ruby's gorgeous home. It wasn't fair. Ruby's mates jumped straight into bed with her, then moved her into a mansion!

Bella's mates almost died bringing her back from the abyss, and brought our dads home to us, too. Men we'd thought were dead or gone forever.

But my mates? I dashed the tears away as Bella walked into the room.

"Tiffany, hey, I... What's wrong?"

I got to my feet, shaking my head. "Oh, nothing... nothing. How's everything with you?"

Bella frowned. "Sit down. Talk to me."

I shook my head again, but let my friend pull me back onto the loveseat anyway. "I'm fine, Bella. Just being silly. We should go in and see Ruby." I made to get up again.

Bella grabbed my hands. "Don't make me cast a truth spell on you," she threatened with a smile. "You know I can do it."

I couldn't help but chuckle at that. "Yeah, I know you can do it." I sighed. "You're going to think I'm ridiculous as well. And I know I am! Ruby's in there, fighting for her life. Our dads are in the backyard, stuck in wolf form. We're linked to some twenty-three-year-old curse that's sucking the life out of the pack. And I'm..."

"Worried about your mates, and how the whole relationship is going to work?" She nodded. "I know. Been there, done that."

I sighed and hunched my shoulders, feeling deflated. "I just feel so selfish."

Bella wrapped her arm around my shoulders and squeezed tight. "You're not selfish at all, Tiff. You're just... impatient. You always have been. You want what you want, now. And there's nothing wrong with that. It drives you forward. I kind of admire that about you."

I sniffed and wiped my nose with my sleeve. "Thanks but telling me that I act like a toddler is not something to admire."

Bella laughed. "Tiff, you are strong, and capable, and loving, and loyal to a fault. Those three guys would be lucky to have you."

"They don't want me." I sniffed. "They want to keep fucking their way around the country, and I'm too... innocent for them."

I'd give them my virginity, the moment they asked for it. I wasn't attached to my sexless state the way Bella had been. I'd wanted it gone years ago. I threw my hands up in the air. "What do you even do with three guys in bed, Bella? I couldn't even handle one."

"You don't know that..."

I jumped to my feet. "Yes, I do." I sniffed and wiped my nose again with my hand, tears burning at the back of my throat. "I never told you guys, but I, well, I..."

Bella got to her feet. "What did you do?"

A hot wash of shame swept over me once more, but for the first time since it happened, I wanted to tell my friend. "I tried to seduce Miles when I was sixteen. You know, the warlock from school?"

Bella's eyes went big and wide. "Okay… what happened?"

"He couldn't… you know…" I indicated to my groin area. "He didn't want me. No matter what I did." As a naïve sixteen-year-old I'd done everything I could think of to get him to want me, but his dick had stayed as flaccid as a sausage from the butcher. *Softer even!*

Bella covered her mouth as though shocked, but there was a smile flirting with the edges of her mouth that made me want to smack her in the face.

"Bella! Don't you dare laugh at me."

"I'm not. I'm not, I promise," Bella said, shaking her head. "It's just that… Miles? Really? He's such a wimp. Totally not your sort of guy *at all.*"

I frowned at her. "He was cute enough. And I wanted a boyfriend. I wanted… someone to love me." Especially since my mom was always working to keep a roof over our heads and my dad had been nonexistent in my life. "I just…" I sighed.

Bella rushed forward and grabbed both my hands. "Tiffany Anderri, are you listening?"

"Yes."

"You are beautiful. You are fierce. And you have saved my life now, multiple times. I trust you with everything I hold dear, and I can tell you with no amount of bias, that you *are* loveable. You and your pack of men will get through whatever challenges you're about to face— together."

I finally forced myself to meet her gaze. "How do you know?"

"Because I have faith. In you. And in our love spell. Our magic would never have called upon three men who weren't perfect for you. Even if you can't see it just yet, I promise everything will work out. It will."

I snorted. "You can't possibly know that, Bell."

She grinned. "But I do. Want me to do a scrying session for you?"

I blinked. Bella had never offered to do one of those for me before, though I knew she was really good at them. "About what? My future?"

She nodded. "Just enough to give you some certainty in moving forward."

A wave of love for my best friend crashed into me. "Really, Bell? Are you sure?"

She nodded and went over to the coffee table, kneeling down in front of it and closing her eyes.

I glanced over toward the kitchen. "Here? Shouldn't we be in with the moms, checking on Ruby?"

She shook her head. "Mom and Rebecca are outside with ours dads. And I think that after the stress of today, we could both use some positive news, don't you?"

She was right there. I walked over and knelt down next to her on the soft carpet.

Bella had her hands out in front of her, wrapped around nothing. Then all of a sudden her scrying ball appeared out of nowhere, and now rested within the circle of her cupped hands.

"Where'd that come from?"

She shrugged. "Just transported it here, from home. It's not far."

I blinked. Bella's magic was *so* much more powerful than mine. "You seem super confident in this," I said to her, my heart pounding a little harder in my chest. Was Bella really going to tell me that everything was going to be fine? That I'd get my happily ever after with the three men Fate had made for me?

Bella closed her eyes and purple magic swirls began to manifest inside the ball. Around and around, it went. Bella focused on the scrying crystal, not speaking aloud.

My stomach dropped and twisted, making me feel sick. *Please let it be all good news.* I glanced toward the kitchen, where the family waited. *We could use some good news about now.*

Bella frowned, the lines between her eyes growing deeper. The smoke in the ball became black and she dropped her hands down, sighing.

"What is it? What did it say?" I asked.

Bella slumped backwards so she ended up sitting on her bum on the carpet.

I crossed my legs and faced her, sitting on the floor with her, my heart in my throat. "Tell me, Bella. What did it say?"

She shook her head. "I can't."

Fear lanced through me like a knife, cutting raw and deep. "Because it's really bad? Something happens to us? Or them? Please tell me something. *Anything*." We'd gone into this scrying session with all the best intentions, or Bella had, but now I felt worse than I had before. *This is probably why she's never done this for me, or anyone I know.* The results were too varied. She had no control over what happened.

"I can't, because the future is too dark to see through it. There's like a black storm cloud headed our way, and my magic can't see past it."

"For me?" I asked, swallowing hard. *It's worse than I thought.*

Bella pinned me with an intense stare, her eyes still shimmering purple with her lingering magic. "For *all* of us."

CHAPTER 8

OLIVER

When the guys told me that Tiffany had pretty much given us an ultimatum, be at a place of her choosing by seven tonight or piss off forever, my initial reaction was pretty bad, if I was honest. I'd said something along the lines of, "tell her to go to hell," and several other choice phrases...

But by the time seven o'clock rolled around, and the other two guys had taken off to meet Tiffany for dinner, I was beginning to have second thoughts. "Fuck. I should be there." I paced along the edge of the forest.

After the other guys had gone back to their parents' places to shower, and shave, I'd gone to the outskirts of town to shift. *To run away.*

Now that I was standing here alone, my temper had cooled, and all I could think about was the possible future I was losing. A wolf shifter only had a single Fated Mate—if we were lucky. If Tiffany was mine, then by turning my back on her, I was turning my back on the only chance of love I was ever going to get. I was basically flushing it down the toilet with a big old 'fuck you' salute.

My only chance of having a home and children. Did I really want to keep traveling? Have no roots. Never know what it was like to raise kids? An aching, tight pain of regret gnawed at my gut. This was my doing. My anger and stubbornness.

There was an intense magic in the air tonight. It couldn't be a coincidence. I could feel it. This was a major turning point in my life and despite my initial reaction of shock, I was beginning to think I'd made a seriously foolish mistake. *What the hell should I do now?*

Town was a fifteen-minute drive away, and I was already late! I started running I'm not sure why I didn't take off toward town in wolf form, but instead I just followed my feet and ran back to the first house we'd visited earlier today. I knocked on the door.

Bella answered with a confused frown on her face. "Ollie, what are you doing here?"

I got straight down to brass tacks. I didn't have time to waste. "I wasn't going to meet Tiffany at the café, but now I'm regretting it."

Elliot strode up behind his mate and slid a possessive hand around her waist. "Hey man. What's up?"

"I need to get into town. To some burger place," I said.

Bella nodded. "Sam's."

"Yeah! But Tiffany said seven, and it's already seven. I need to be there."

Bella grinned. "Worried you're going to miss out on having a powerful witch as your mate?"

"I... hadn't even thought much about the witch thing," I said, being honest. "I think I was more shocked that I had a mate, *at all*. I'd kind of gotten my head around the fact that it was never going to happen for me —for us." And part of me had been okay with that. *A very small part of me.* The part of me that had resigned itself to a life spent in the company of my two best friends... because that's all there was. Hoping for any more had been akin to emotional suicide. Daring to hope was a path that led to heartbreak and until now, I hadn't thought hope worth the risk. *Not really.*

Elliot chuckled. "Yeah, I thought that too until Bella came along." He wrapped both arms around his mate's waist and cuddled her openly. Such public displays of affection weren't super common around here. Especially for Alphas.

"I don't want to break this up, but can you call her? Or can I borrow a car?"

Bella's eyes lit up and she grinned. "I can do you one better."

A shiver of worry coursed down my back. "What can you do?"

"I can send you straight to her via magic, but I have to warn you that most wolves feel sick the first time they're transported."

I clenched my teeth. If feeling sick was the price to get back on track with my mate? I'd pay it a thousand times over. "Okay. Do it."

"Come in. Quickly," Bella said.

I followed them inside.

Elliot patted me on the back. "Take a teaspoon of cement and harden the fuck up, mate. These girls are worth the hassle," he said before He stepped away.

I faced the witch. "Go for it, Bella. And thank you."

She smiled. "Just try not to stuff it up once you get there, okay?" With a flick of her hand, white sparkles hit me...

And *zip!* I was suddenly standing next to a table, inside of a warm restaurant. I blinked, my stomach twisting and turning like I was about to vomit.

"Ollie!" Tiffany cried from her place, sitting in one of the café booths. "Where'd you come from?"

"I... um..." I tried to grab for the table nearest to me before I fell over, but my legs buckled beneath me. Instead of focusing on the pain in my shoulder as I hit the concrete floor, I simply focused on not throwing up. *Swallow. Just swallow.* I gulped. *Stay down.* I coached the contents of my stomach. "Whoa." I stayed where I fell, though hands from above grabbed for me to pull me up. I waved them off. "Give me a second. I just need to stay here for a sec."

"He'll be better in a minute," Tiffany said.

And I was. Within a few heartbeats, the nausea began to recede. Strength returned to my arms and legs, and I slowly pushed myself to my feet and brushed off whatever dust and grime I'd picked up from the floor.

Tiffany grinned at me. "So much for not making a scene."

I glanced around. Everyone in the small restaurant was whispering and staring. "Lucky it's not busy. May I join you?"

Tiff was sitting by herself on one side of the booth, with Fin and Jase sitting opposite her. Why they chose to sit so far away, I didn't know. She nodded.

I slid straight into the booth next to her, sliding my hand over her thigh.

She jumped at my touch, electricity sizzling between us.

And I reveled in her reaction. "I'm sorry I'm late," I said, though a possessive growl rose in my throat.

She swallowed visibly, but she didn't move my hand away. In fact, she seemed to slide a little closer. "It's okay. I kind of figured you weren't going to make it."

"Yeah, me too. But you know... Fate called." I grinned at her, and her eyes shone at me as she stared at me, then she cleared her throat. "You traveled by magic to get here. So, I have to assume Bella helped you?"

I nodded.

She slid her hand over mine, where it rested on her thigh, but instead of pushing my hand away like I expected, she curled her fingers around mine, holding my hand in place. "That was very brave of you. I know transportation spells knock shifters around a bit."

I shrugged. "It was worth it. I would have kicked myself a thousand times over if I'd missed out on tonight."

Fin and Jase stared at me like I'd grown a second ass. "What?" they blurted in unison, before they shook their heads and grabbed the menus in front of them like they'd been snapped out of a trance.

I turned in my seat to stare at my mate. She was glowing. Her skin. Her gorgeous blonde hair. Her bright blue eyes. "You look beautiful."

She blushed, hot and red.

I chuckled. "Now you're even more beautiful."

She glanced down at the table as though embarrassed, then looked up at me through her thick, black eyelashes.

Desire flourished in my belly, deep and dark. I couldn't stop myself from reaching for her face and pulling her toward me. She was mine. I couldn't wait to taste her.

When our lips met, we both gasped at the sensation.

It was as tingly as fireworks exploding inside my skin, and as sweet as caramelized sugar all at once.

She melted into me.

I pulled her closer, pressing my lips hard against hers in a possessive kiss that I hoped showed her exactly what I wanted to do to her later. Virgin or not, she was ours. And I wasn't going to hold back. When I finally lifted my head, I stared down into her eyes and fell into them. She was heat, and light, and everything that was good in this world.

I swooped down for another kiss, this time tasting her with my tongue.

Someone nearby cleared their throat, and the noise finally broke through the cloud surrounding me.

I pulled back.

Tiffany giggled a little, pressing her fingers to her lips as though to stifle the noise—or imprint my kiss on her mouth forever.

"Who's hungry?" I asked, picking up the menu and forcing my gaze to the words I couldn't quite focus on just yet. My cock was throbbing, hard and persistent beneath the table. I wanted to grab my mate and strip us both naked so I could have my way with her. But I needed to keep a lid on it. At least for now.

While I stared at the menu, not caring one whit what I was about to eat, I had to think about where we were going to take Tiff tonight.

None of us had our own place. We'd planned on crashing at our parents' houses while we were here, but I wanted to take our mate somewhere we could seduce her. My old bedroom, with my king single bed and my parents in the next room, was *not* the way to do it.

"What made you change your mind?" Fin asked. "I didn't think you wanted to be part of this... family."

I glanced up at my friend, a guy I'd known my whole life, and for the first time noticed the hurt there. Had he thought I was rejecting *him*? That was weird. "I figured Fate doesn't fuck things up, but I was going to if I didn't get my ass over here."

"So, you believe we're Fated Mates now?" Tiffany asked. "That we will end up living together, and all that stuff?"

I tried to repress my immediate reaction to the whole, 'married with kids' thing. It was such a cliché. And as a family of four, surely we could break the rules a little? Make a future that we all wanted. *Something unique.*

"Yeah, I do believe it," I admitted, and swallowed against the thickness in my throat. "I think the problem was... I never expected to find a mate at all, period. I'd talked myself into believing I'd be single forever. So, when you showed up, and I had that intense, 'I need to fuck you right now', reaction... What's wrong?"

Tiffany had practically choked on her water, coughing and spluttering into her napkin.

Fin groaned. "She's a virgin, Ollie. You can't say things like that."

She shook her head, coughing to clear her throat. "No. You can. I just... I'm not used to it, that's all. I'm not made of glass."

"Yeah, what happened there?" Fin asked, perplexed. "The guys around here blind or something?"

She smiled at the compliment and tilted her head. "Well, Ruby, Bella, and I made a pact a few years ago after we found the spell book. The one that showed us how to call our soul mates to us. None of us wanted to play around. We just wanted one guy—the right guy. So, we all swore that we'd wait until after the spell was cast, so then we wouldn't get hurt."

"Get hurt?" I asked, frowning in confusion. *Is sex really that painful for a girl?*

"We all grew up with mothers who'd been abandoned by our fathers, or so they thought at the time. None of our moms ever dated again after we were born. And they obviously didn't remarry or have other kids. It was sad, seeing our moms so lonely and depressed. It put us off dating. We just wanted the right one."

"That's understandable," I said, glancing over at Fin and Jase.

We couldn't relate to that sort of upbringing, ourselves. Our parents had all mated young, and stayed together, forever. Break ups within wolf pairings were as rare as hens' teeth. But I could imagine that having her sort of childhood would have changed how she saw life. And marriage. And men.

"Plus," Tiffany went on. "None of the guys around us were interested in dating us anyway. We thought it had something to do with our moms being single, but now we know it was probably our wolf shifter blood. The warlocks our age didn't want us, and the humans practically ran in the opposite direction..." She shrugged, but pain crossed her face.

I slid my hand onto her thigh again, as close to her pussy as I dared and squeezed gently.

She jumped a little, casting a furtive glance my way.

"Their loss," I said. "I'm sorry for being a fuckwit before. About the whole virginity thing. That was stupid."

She bit her lip. "Yeah, well, I thought it was a bit weird. But as long as you guys are okay about it now?"

"As long as you're not attached to it, because I'm hoping to part you with it as soon as possible."

"Oh, um... yeah." She glanced across the table. "All three of you want to do that, right?"

"Hell yes," Jase said.

Fin grinned. "Of course. As soon as you're ready to mate with us, I'm in. I can't speak for the other guys, but I've been waiting for you for a decade, Tiff."

Tiffany smiled at him, flashing her brilliant white teeth. "That's a long time."

I slid my little finger even closer to the juncture of her thighs, watching heat flush her beautiful cheeks. "Yes, it is."

She grabbed my hand, holding it a couple of inches away from its destination. "Well, it's all yours. But should we eat dinner first?"

I laughed aloud at that one. This girl was so much more innocent than she appeared. I had to remember that. She was sweet in a way I'd never appreciated in a woman before. "Yes, gorgeous. We can wait until after dinner."

No point losing her virginity on an empty stomach, after all.

I couldn't wait to claim her, but how we were going to do this, all three of us sharing a single woman, God only knew!

CHAPTER 9

TIFFANY

I spent the entirety of dinner wriggling in my seat, trying to keep my head above the waves of arousal that hit me every time I caught the lust in my mates' gazes. And when I wasn't trying to distract myself from how uncomfortable and *hot* under the collar, they were making me, I was laughing at their antics.

They were all gorgeous—but in totally different ways.

Ollie was assertive, sarcastic, and had a dirty way of talking that both embarrassed me and turned me on at the same time. He had short dark hair and incredibly dark eyes that made me want to stare into their depths to try and discover his secrets.

Fin on the other hand was relaxed, and sweet, and almost too beautiful to look at. He had tanned skin, bright blue eyes, and dirty blond hair that fell all the way down to his shoulders. He was better looking than me!

And Jase? Well, he made me shift in my seat the most. He was funny, and lovely, and had an edgy hardness to his looks that made me think he'd be great in bed.

That was one of the things I loved about having mates older than me. Although I hated the idea of them having had so many women before me—in fact, the jealousy made me sick if I dwelled too much upon it—I loved that they'd know what they were doing. Our first time, *my* first time, wouldn't be two ridiculous teenagers fumbling in the dark, with no discernable idea about what either one should be doing.

And thank God they knew what they were doing, because I certainly didn't. If anything, I was intensely afraid I was going to disappoint them. The only guy I'd ever tried to seduce had found me to be the biggest turnoff. Those memories had haunted me for years, and I was pretty sure that if my mates ended up having the same reaction to my touch, I would absolutely die of shame.

We finished our meals and paid. Then it was time to get up and leave the warmth of the familiar restaurant. I didn't have to be home by any specific time tonight. I didn't have a curfew at my age and my mom knew where I was, but I had no idea what the guys wanted to do.

"Do you three want to see my house?" I asked, aiming for as casual a tone of voice as possible. "Or are we calling it a night now?"

The three men exchanged glances.

Then Fin turned to me, his face as serious as a seizure. "We don't have a house like Ruby's and Bella's mates. We'd planned on just staying at our parents' houses over Christmas, then heading off again."

"Um... okay." I frowned at them. What did that have to do with our plans for the night? "That didn't answer my question."

The guys exchanged glances again.

"What we mean is, we don't have the money to offer you the immediate home and future the other guys did for their mates." Jase finally said, his lips twisted as though he was annoyed.

I opened my mouth to answer, but he rushed to interrupt me.

"But we will. We'll all get jobs and rent a place to start with. Then we'll save up for a home for you. We'll be the mates you deserve, Tiffany. We promise."

Ah, so that's what the problem is! I smiled at them. I didn't care about those things. All I wanted was a man, or in this case, three men, who actually wanted me. The rest would take care of itself in the long term, like it did for all partnerships. "Well, I might have a solution to that in the short term. Are you guys up for a bit of a walk?"

Ollie's eyebrows drew down into a frown, but he ended up nodding. "Okay. Yeah, sure."

I led them along the main street and through the town, chatting the whole time about family and life. Nothing too serious.

We laughed the whole way.

Ruby and Bella knew about this secret of mine, but as someone who didn't like to talk about money, it wasn't something I casually told many people. When we finally reached a little town house with a white picket fence, I stood proudly in front of it, beaming at them.

"What's this?" Jase asked, glancing up at the house.

"Is this where you and your mom live?" Fin asked.

I shook my head with a grin. "Nope! This is *my* place."

"What do you mean?" Ollie said, sounding confused. "I thought you lived with your mom?"

"I do," I said with a sigh. "Long story short. I wasn't very good at school, so got out as soon as possible and went straight to work as a hairdresser. I lived with my mom and didn't have a lot of expenses, so when I had the down payment, I bought this place." I indicated the property I'd bought at just nineteen years old.

"It's been leased out since I bought it, and it's only got two bedrooms, so it's not huge or anything. But if you guys would help me pay the mortgage off, because I can't afford to do it on my own, then we could live here together. Then maybe, after a while, we could get something bigger? Maybe something closer to the pack if you want?"

I had no idea if they'd want to live in town with me. Wolf shifters and humans didn't mix very well, but it was the best option I could see. My tenants had been making noise about moving out soon anyway, and instead of re-leasing it I could move us in, and we'd have an instant home for our new little family.

Now that I thought about it, with the way the bedrooms were arranged next to each other, we could even knock out the dividing wall between the two and make it one big bedroom. If that was what they wanted...

I didn't want to tell them my plans out loud. They seemed a little gun-shy when it came to talking about the future. Or had, up until just now. They seemed to be coming around to the idea of us being together. Slowly, but surely.

"Are you serious?" Ollie said, his mouth dropping open.

I frowned at him. "Ah, yeah. Why?"

He chuckled loudly. "Because it's fucking awesome! How... how did you do this?"

I shrugged. "I work hard."

They all grinned at me.

"Looks like we're the ones that are going to have to lift our game, huh boys?" Ollie said.

The other two shook their heads and laughed in agreement.

Ollie grabbed me and swung me up into his arms. "Looks like you have the future sorted, gorgeous. But we need somewhere to take you tonight. Is there a motel nearby?"

A shiver of premonition moved through me. *Yes. This was the right path for me.* "Ah, yes," I said, running my fingers up his arms and loving the feeling of his strong muscles beneath my palms. "There's two, I think. The nicer one is a block or so from here."

I knew most people in town, and we'd probably start an absolute firestorm of gossip if anyone saw me going into a motel with three hunky guys, but I couldn't stop the shiver of excitement that passed through me at the thought.

Ollie's dark eyes lit up. "Lead the way."

He took my hand and I managed to walk calmly, without screaming, all the way to the motel.

Mercifully, the guy behind the desk was a stranger, an amazing thing in a town as small as ours, and we got the biggest room they had. The clerk looked at us weirdly but didn't question Fin when he handed over some cash and took the key card. In fact, the guy looked a touch scared if anything.

Humans had issues with shifters, and it was obvious as the guy paled that my three wolves had him feeling beyond his normal levels of inadequacy.

We went up to the room and shut the door.

My stomach was all knotted up and there was an aching pulse deep in my belly that I couldn't ignore. I was fifty percent nerves and anxiety, and fifty percent excitement and horniness. It was a heady and dizzying combination.

Ollie reached for me first.

I put a hand up to his chest, pressing against it, hard enough to stop him. I needed to get something off my chest first. "Thank you for coming to the restaurant tonight. I know I was pushy with what I said about you having to be there and everything. I shouldn't have been like that."

Mom had made me see clearly just how petty I'd been. Just because I'd been waiting for them, and technically they'd been looking for me, hadn't meant they were as prepared for the 'till death do us part' bit as I was. Especially since they had to share me.

Ollie slid his hands around my waist, then grabbed my ass and hauled me into his body.

I gasped, heat bursting to life in my core like a flower unfurling.

The hardness beneath his jeans pressed against me.

I almost moaned at the feel, relief sweeping through me. I wasn't going to be disappointed tonight. *This time will be different.*

"I shouldn't have been so resistant to what Fate had planned for me," Ollie said, then ducked his head and kissed the side of my neck.

I melted into him.

He nipped and sucked his way up the column of my throat. "You're meant for us, and we're meant for you. And it's time we made you ours."

His whispered words were everything I'd ever wanted to hear, and I closed my eyes against the wave of arousal that swept over me.

He slid his hands up underneath the back of my top.

I cupped his face, drawing his mouth to mine. A moan escaped my lips as a tingle of awareness passed over me. It wasn't as strong or as strange as the first time we'd touched, but it was still there, letting me know that I'd made the right choice. That this man, this shifter, was one of the incredible men made just for me.

Ollie swept his tongue into my mouth, surprising me with the growl that rolled through him.

I pulled back, feeling the eyes of the other two guys upon me. With a coy grimace, I grabbed hold of Ollie's hand, so I didn't get disconnected from him, and looked at Fin and Jase. "I need to have a quick bathroom break; then can we have a chat about how this is going to happen? I'm a little bit nervous about the whole, three guys on one girl… thing."

Ollie chuckled. "We've never done this before either, so I think we're going to need to feel our way through things."

"Let's check out the bathroom," Jase said, walking through the large room and opening the ensuite door. He turned back to me with a grin. "If you want some privacy for a minute, go for it, but after you're done, I could really use a shower. The other guys too. So, do you want to watch us for a bit first? Get comfortable with us before we take you to bed?"

My mouth dropped open. "All three of you are going to shower, together?" I was going to get to look at them naked, together, like… now? I wasn't really prepared for that. But then, was I prepared for any of this craziness Fate had dealt me?

Jase nodded, then pretended to sniff his friend. "Ollie needs a shower more than me."

"Hey!" Ollie swatted at him, then shrugged sheepishly. "It is true."

Jase tilted his head toward the bathroom. "The shower is massive. So, you go do whatever you've got to do and when you're ready, we'll all come have a quick shower and wash the day off."

"More like the past *week*," Fin said with a grin. "We've been running for days to come home to you."

I shivered, loving their expressions and the fact they were giving me this time to get more comfortable—and to ramp up the heat and tension before getting into bed together. *Best foreplay ever!* I gave them a grin, then ducked into the bathroom and shut the door behind me.

Oh my god! *Bloody, wow.* This was really happening.

CHAPTER 10

TIFFANY

I pressed my forehead against the closed door and shut my eyes. This was really happening. After practically ten years of wondering what my first time would be like, who it would be with, and how it would go... I now had the answer. My first time was going to be with three men who were destined to be mine, and who I was going to see completely naked, in this bathroom, in about five minutes.

I could barely breathe with the excitement saturating every part of me.

"You okay in there?" someone called out.

I think it was Fin. "Yeah. Yeah. All good," I called back, pushing myself up and turning around to check out this supposedly massive bathroom.

Jase was right. The ensuite was more like a wet room, with floor-to-ceiling tiles, one large glass panel separating the shower from the room, and two large shower heads so at least two people could shower at once. *Probably more.*

I bit my lip and shivered as a sense of true longing rippled through me. I'd never be alone again. I wondered if I'd ever truly wrap my head around that concept. *I have my mates!* I could almost scream.

I hurried to finish my bathroom necessities, then stripped off to take a quick shower myself. If they were going to be kissing, and licking, and smelling me in all of those places... I wanted to be as fresh as possible. I needed every bit of body confidence I could get in front of these three gorgeous, more experienced guys!

When I was warm, clean, and dry, I glanced around the bathroom. I didn't really want to put on the clothes I'd been wearing to dinner. It felt wrong after washing myself so thoroughly. So, I grabbed the fluffy white robe that was hanging on the back of the door and slipped it on.

It wasn't exactly fancy lingerie, but it would give the guys easy access at least. After I tied the belt around the robe, I opened the door and met Fin's eyes. "All done," I said cheerfully.

He grinned back at me. "Great." Then he began to pull off his clothes.

I glanced away, getting more and more embarrassed with each article of clothing that disappeared. I tried to find somewhere to look that wouldn't make the heat climb further up my face, but everywhere my gaze landed, there was a naked man. *Holy shit!*

Ollie, Jase, and Fin had all completely stripped, and they sauntered forward to come into the bathroom,

I hurried back, dragging the door open with me.

Fin swaggered in, all big shoulders and awesome six-pack. "Hey," he said with a grin as he walked into the shower and flicked on the water.

Jase was next. He was huge in every way; shoulders, arms, even his cock was so long it made me look away, mortified to be staring.

Ollie slid an arm around my waist and tugged me into him.

I squealed when my hands came up to press against his huge, hot pecs. "Whoa."

He chuckled and kissed me quickly on the mouth, then strode over to the shower and stood at the opening, waiting his turn.

I bit my lip and glanced at the floor, the white tiles beneath my feet. My stomach tightened with both excitement and arousal, and there was the most incredible pull to look at my men. I knew I was allowed to, and they wanted me to, but I'd literally never seen a naked man in real life before. My teenage experience with the warlock had been in the dark, and I'd been the one to turn off the lights. I hadn't wanted to see all his dirty, ugly private bits.

Curiosity eventually got the better of me and I lifted my head to peep at the men washing themselves in the shower. My mouth dropped open, and my heart started to pound with a whole new level of arousal. *Oh. My. God.* They were fucking beautiful! Their bodies were all sculpted and made of pure muscle. They looked strong, and lithe and hot, all at once—like a team of Olympian gods.

Ollie grinned at me as he scrubbed his body with suds, then stepped beneath the water and washed the soap away. "We won't be long, gorgeous girl. Unless you want to join us in here?"

I opened my mouth to respond, then just shook my head, more embarrassed now. I would have loved to say I had the confidence to throw off the robe and strut into the shower like a boss to join them. Maybe even make love to them in there, with my back pressed against the cold tiles and my head beneath the warm water.

I shivered, my pussy throbbing in dire need. "I'm, ah..." I couldn't finish the sentence, and I couldn't stop staring at them. I was trapped by their beauty, as if drawn in by their gravity.

They flicked off the water and began to grab towels, the water droplets running down their exquisite bodies, their wet hair hanging over their eyes in a deliciously feral and rogue way.

I licked my lips, my mouth suddenly dry. *How is this real?*

They moved toward me...

And I bolted into the bedroom. Out of the frying pan and into the fire. "Um..." I didn't know what to say or what to do. How did you even start a session like the one we were about to have?

Ollie reached for my hand and tugged me toward him. "Don't think, gorgeous. Just feel how right this all is." He cupped my face and pulled me into him for a kiss.

I closed my eyes, slid my hands up his chest to wrap my arms around his neck, and gave myself over to the storm of passion sweeping me up. This was my future, my fate. And hopefully the path to break the curse and give us back the lives we were always meant to have.

Jase grabbed for the robe at my shoulders.

Ollie undid the knot in the belt around my waist.

I broke the kiss and leaned back.

Jase peeled the robe down my arms.

And Ollie pulled back to stare down at my naked body, a dark hunger evident in his eyes. "Fuck, you're more beautiful than I even imagined you would be."

Every part of me screamed that I needed to cover up, to raise my arms and hide my body from Ollie's view. But I didn't. That would have undermined everything we were trying to build. They desired me. They wanted to look. So, I lifted my chin and let him stare at me, trying to bury the anxiety and embarrassment that threatened to consume me.

That's when Jase grabbed my hand and spun me around so he could look his fill as well.

I struggled not to reach for the robe that had dropped to the floor, once again feeling vulnerable under my mate's stare. But as my gaze caught on his heavy, thick erection, I swallowed down my squeal of embarrassment and instead focused on their need for me.

Then Jase dragged me into his arms for my first kiss with him.

I moaned as my pelvis cradled his narrow hips, and my breasts pressed against his chest.

Jase grabbed me by the waist and lifted me.

I clung to his shoulders and wrapped my legs around his hips as he walked me to the bed.

He rolled onto the soft surface and landed on top of me.

I couldn't stop all of my focus going straight to the way his cock poked into my belly. I looked over his shoulder at the other two, obscenely staring at the way their cocks jutted out from their bodies also. The relief I felt was palpable. I grinned and went back to kissing Jase, but he stopped and stared at me strangely. "What were you looking at just then?"

"Um…"

He nipped my jaw with his teeth. "You can tell us the truth. Always, gorgeous."

I shook my head. "I was just looking at the other guys. That's all."

He chuckled. "There was something in your face I couldn't quite decipher. What was it? Is it fear? Are you scared about tonight?"

"No, it's not that." I sighed. I didn't want to get into it, but they may as well know the real truth about me and the reasons I had the hang-ups I did. "There was one guy I dated for a little while in high school, when I was sixteen. And when we were fooling around, he couldn't, you know, get it up. He said it was my fault. That I was repulsive and ugly." I swallowed the lump in my throat as I practically spat the words out, wanting to be rid of them once for all.

Jase's eyebrows climbed his forehead, then he began to pull back and get off me.

I grabbed for him, horrified that he would leave me after I'd revealed such a private and painful thing to him. "No, please. Don't go!" I panicked. "I didn't mean to upset you."

Jase laughed. "I'm not leaving, sweetheart. Not in a million years. I just wanted to show you that we don't have *that* issue." He stood next to Ollie and grinned at me. "Look your fill, sweetheart."

I sat up on the bed and looked from face to face. They were deadly serious. They were happy for me to just stare at them to my heart's content. "Really?"

Ollie grunted. "Fuck yeah. Go for it."

I slid to the edge of the bed and studied them, from their intense eyes to their long, hard cocks, all lined up and ready for me.

Ollie grinned then charged toward me. "I hope that's enough for now, because it's our turn to love on you." He pushed me back onto the bed and kneeled on the floor between my legs, spreading my thighs open.

"What are you doing?" I cried out in shock.

The other two slid onto the bed with me.

Ollie stared up at my face. "I'm making sure you're so hot and wet for me, by the time I slide into you, you'll be begging me for it."

Oh, my God. I covered my face with my hands and lay back on the bed, mortified. I couldn't handle him talking like that, saying those sorts of words to me. But at the same time, they circled around and around in my head, easing the pain of the past and cementing the path to the future.

Fin slid his hands over my breasts and nipples.

I dropped my hands to stare up at him. I couldn't hide from this—from them.

Jase turned my face toward him and started kissing me.

I cried out against his lips as I felt Ollie's tongue slide down my pussy. His groans of pleasure broke me. And I cried out again as his tongue thrust inside me. "Oh, fuck!" I moaned, arching my back and loving every second of what they were doing to me.

I was being kissed, touched, licked, and sucked from every conceivable angle. Three mouths were on me. Three sets of loving, knowledgeable hands. There was nothing to do but moan with ecstasy and let them have their way with me. This is what I'd waited for, for so long...

By the time Ollie climbed up between my thighs to lay on top of me, I was a shivering pile of pulsing, triggered nerve endings, unable to do anything but focus on how good everything felt. And how much better it was going to be when Ollie finally appeased the ache throbbing deep in my belly.

"You ready for me?" he whispered into my ear as he pressed his weight down upon me.

I wrapped my thighs around his waist and bucked up at him, needing something to ease the ache inside me. I nodded, biting my bottom lip hard. *I'm ready.*

Ollie pushed himself up on his hands.

I grabbed for his back, trying to drag him back down again. "Please."

"Please what?" he asked, his gaze intense.

I tilted my hips as invitingly as I could. I wanted—needed—to cum so bad.

Ollie tilted his head and I saw the same stubbornness that others saw in me. He wanted me to say it. He was going to make me spell it out. He was going to make me beg, just as he said.

I swallowed down my stupid embarrassed pride. "*Please* fuck me."

A growl sounded from around me, above me, within me, and the wolf shifter on top of me, my mate, bent his head to consume me with a kiss.

When my mate said those three magic words, I almost blew all over her belly like some teenage kid who couldn't hold his load. My wolf howled inside my head, and I had to stop, clench my jaw, and force him back into the recesses of my mind.

I would not do anything to hurt Tiffany, and that meant keeping my wolf locked up tight. She wasn't ready for that. Not yet. It was her first time... So, I grabbed my cock and rubbed my flesh along her slit, then up to tap the head against her clit.

She cried out, arching her back and digging her nails into my arms. "Please..." she begged; her voice tinged with a sweet note of desperation. "*Ollie...*"

I was only human after all. I set my cock at her entrance and nudged the head inside. Hot, wet heat engulfed me, and I groaned, thrusting forward as slowly as I could, considering my lust was riding me hard as the damn Devil, like an inferno at my back.

I paused, waiting a moment for her to adjust to me. She was barely breathing as I slid into her and the last thing I wanted to do was hurt her. But from what I'd heard, there would be a little pain, no matter how gentle I was. So, I kissed her neck and rocked my hips forward slowly, sinking deeper and deeper. Then I surged forward with one final push.

A soft cry of pain whispered from her lips and her eyes closed.

I was fully seated inside her, my flesh to hers. I rested my body carefully on hers so that I could whisper in her ear. "Are you okay, gorgeous?"

She nodded against my face and gripped me tight, both with her hands, and inside where my cock was hard and ready for more. She opened her eyes and met my gaze. "Yes. Please don't stop. I need you."

Growling as I began to move, I slid in and out of her as she gasped with every hilt-deep thrust of my cock into her luscious pussy. I fucked harder and faster, riding her until she was screaming for me. I held on so tight to the reins of control, I had to clench my fists against the sheets and bite my own knuckle to stop from coming before her.

When I heard her breath hitch, felt her back arch, then her pussy clamp down on me, I cried out with relief as I pumped into her.

She came all over my cock.

And I reveled in the magical feeling, finally able to let myself go as my own orgasm crashed over me with a breath-taking brutality I've never experienced before. I dropped my head and instinctively bit into the soft flesh of her shoulder as I pulsed my seed into her, claiming her. *My mate.*

"Oh, my God. That was amazing," Tiffany whispered.

I finally lifted my head and kissed her softly on the lips. She could say that again. My head was still spinning. I grinned. "You had enough? Or...?" I glanced to the side of her, where my two best friends waited for their chance to be with our mate.

"We can wait if you're sore," Fin said, always the gentleman.

I withdrew from her and slid off the bed to stand up. My legs wobbled and I ended up sitting on the end of the bed.

Tiffany looked from one of them to the other, her expression one of worry.

I wasn't sure why. "Are you sore?" I asked gently. "Or are you afraid of rejecting them? It's okay. You can be honest with us. We're not going to force you."

She sat up, shaking her head. "No. It's not that. Not at all. I... would love... more. If that's okay? I just didn't know how they felt about, you know... I mean, they just watched me make love to you."

I grinned and glanced at my friends. "Tell her." I wasn't blind. I could see how aroused they still were. Our mating hadn't done anything to dim their desire.

"Come here," Jase said, drawing Tiff closer to him, before taking her and rolling her over so he was positioned on top of her.

I sat and watched as, one after the other, Jase and Fin made love to Tiff. I'd assumed it would cause a panic within me, an unshakeable anger and jealousy. But my wolf was sated and pleased. Watching Tiffany receive more love, and more pleasure, was shockingly satisfying to me and my inner wolf. She would always be loved and cared for now. Even if we weren't around—she'd always have one or more of us. And I knew my best friends like the back of my hand. They'd look after her if it ever came down to it.

When finally everyone had mated, the room went quiet and still.

I tilted my head at Tiff.

She was lying provocatively on her back, her chest rising and falling rapidly as she struggled to catch her breath.

"How are you feeling, gorgeous girl?"

She groaned, pulling herself up to a seated position. "Guilty as all hell," she said with a grin. "Here I am enjoying myself with you three, and Ruby's at home fighting for her bloody life."

I frowned. "You're going to have to explain that to us. I don't think we ever got the entire story."

She ran a hand through her disheveled hair. "Well, basically, we found out a month or so ago that the old High Warlock of our Coven had used our mothers to put a curse on your pack, so that no-one would ever be able to sire a daughter, and as as a result the pack's line would die out."

My jaw dropped open. "Fucking... what? Where's that old bastard now?"

She cringed. "He's dead, actually. He died last year, which takes me to the even more horrible part. Around Thanksgiving, someone put a curse on the three of us—Ruby, Bella, and me. We all ended up in a magical coma, and well, long story short, we found out it was some of the current members of the witch council who was conducting the curse."

"I hope they got theirs." Fin growled, his eyes flashing.

Tiffany sighed. "Not really, unfortunately. The other boys did their best, but they escaped. We all came out of it in the end, but the worst part is that one of the witches told us that the old High Warlock had grounded the original spell in us—Ruby, Bella, and me."

"Grounded?" Jase asked. "What's that mean exactly?"

I was glad he asked, because I sure as hell didn't know.

"It means that we can't break the spell unless all three of us die. It's connected to our very lives."

My mouth dropped open.

"No fucking way!" Jase said.

My thoughts exactly.

Tiffany laughed. "Yeah, I know. It's insane. So, Bella is hoping that we can break the curse another way—by me mating with you three. Now that we're mated, it means all three of us witches are connected to the pack, and hopefully the curse can be done away with."

"What's with Ruby then?" I asked, still confused about how everything fitted together.

Tiffany's lips trembled. "Ruby's pregnancy is slowly killing her, according to our moms, but ultimately, it's all linked to the spell. Ruby's managed to conceive a girl, which she wasn't meant to be able to. But as she's part of the spell, it seems that she and her daughter are trying to break it on their own... but it's not working. The spell is far too strong, so they've put Ruby into a magical coma to try and buy us a few more days to see if we can break the damn thing once and for all."

"And if you can't find another way around it...?" Jase asked.

"Then they'll have to try and get rid of the baby," Tiff said, her eyes shimmering with unshed tears. "Which will destroy Ruby when she wakes up. She'd never forgive us, any of us, if we let our moms go through with it. But..."

I wrapped my arm around her shoulders and pulled her into my body.

She cuddled in closer, sighing against my chest, clearly needing comfort.

Now, I understood the pressure she felt to make sure everything went smoothly with us. Tiffany had her best friend's mortality on her mind. "That's a shit choice," I said, not able to make it sound pretty. Choosing between a best friend and her child wasn't a decision I'd want to give to my worst enemy. It was cruelty incarnate.

She nodded against my shoulder. "Yeah, it is, but we can't lose Ruby. We can't."

I kissed the top of her head. "You won't."

Jase reached over and squeezed her arm. "Yeah, let's hope that we've just broken the spell. You're mated, so are Ruby and Bella. And all to wolves of the pack that were cursed in the first place, so you never know. Don't give up hope, yet Tiff."

Tiffany sat up. "You're right! We should go back home and see how everyone is." She got to her feet, looking excited.

I shook my head, reaching for her hand with a wry smile. "It's past eleven now, gorgeous. How about we all have showers and get a decent night's sleep? Then first thing in the morning we can head back to the pack grounds and see how your friend is faring."

She stared at me, as though weighing my words. "You're probably right. I'll just message my mom and ask her how Ruby is and let her know I'm not coming home." She headed off to find her cell phone.

I watched her gorgeous ass move as she walked away. *Damn, I could just bite that...*

"How are we doing the bed?" Jase asked.

I frowned at him. "What do you mean?"

He gestured to the two large king beds separated by a small table.

"I'm not sleeping without Tiffany," I said.

"Neither am we," said the other two guys.

Tiffany walked back over, still naked and glorious. Her cheeks were pink, her nipples tight and perky. Every part of her was just crying out to be loved all over again. "Can't we just move that table out of the way and push the beds together?" she asked. "That's what Ruby's mates do, I think. They have two king beds connected. Then we can all sleep together."

I pulled our clever mate into my side, her soft skin against me making me ache for her once more. "Sounds like a plan."

We got straight to work.

Jase lifted the small bedside table out.

Then Fin pushed the two beds together.

Tiffany giggled as she crawled across one giant bed and climbed beneath the sheets.

I jumped onto the same bed that she had and slid beneath the covers, pulling her close.

The other two guys got in too.

Fin huffed over the fact he was the furthest away. "I can't even touch her."

"Fine. Try this," Jase said, pulling Tiffany over to him, then rolling her up so that she was lying on his chest facing up.

I shuffled nearer, reaching for her belly.

Fin rolled closer as well.

Tiffany looked from me to Fin, then back again. Then she laughed, a purely happy, sweet sound that a part of me wanted to memorize and remember always. "You know I'm not going to be able to sleep like this, right?" she said, grinning at me, but not moving to get off Jase, nor stopping anyone from touching her.

"Yeah. That's fine," I said.

"Just give us a few minutes," Jase pleaded from beneath her.

"Fine by me," Tiffany said, nestling in. "I've been waiting for you guys for forever. I can wait for sleep. I've had a lifetime of that."

I frowned. There she was talking about waiting for us, like she was old and on the shelf, which she was nowhere near being. "I'm not trying to be rude or anything, gorgeous, but aren't you, like, only twenty-two?"

Tiffany jutted her chin out. "Yeah, so?"

"So," Fin began gently, "we're all thirty-ish. We've been waiting for you for a *lot* longer that you've been waiting for us. So why does it sound like you think twenty-two is old to find your mates?"

She frowned, her brow furrowing in the middle in the cutest way.

I wanted to reach over and use my thumb to massage the stress away.

"You're right. I suppose it's not long compared to a woman in her thirties, or whatever. I've just wanted a husband since I was young. Too young, you guys would think, and I just..." She sighed, shifting as though she was uncomfortable. "I feel like my life can finally begin now. That probably doesn't make sense to you three."

I chuckled and rolled onto my back, tucking a hand beneath my head and staring up at the ceiling. "You have to remember how we grew up, gorgeous. By the time we were eighteen, it was obvious there was something wrong with the pack. There hadn't been a female born in over a decade, and although we'd grown up with a lot of girls, they all got married off to their mates and we were left standing, so to speak."

"We'd kind of gotten our heads around the fact that we'd never find a mate," Jase said quietly.

"Especially after a year of searching the country," Fin added.

Tiffany looked from me to Jase and back again. "So, you're saying..."

I turned onto my side again to face her. "I suppose we're saying forgive us if we're a bit slow on the uptake. You are a *huge* surprise to us, Tiffany. Actually, scratch that. You are literally a miracle to us."

Tiffany's eyes lit up and she smiled brightly at me, before her smile faded. "What will be a miracle is if we can save Ruby and her baby and bring our dads back from their cursed wolf forms."

"Come here, gorgeous." I pulled her from Jase's chest, and rolled her perfect naked body away from me so I could spoon in behind and her other mates could reach for her too.

I leaned forward, whispering into her ear. "I know there's a lot of other stressors in your life, but for tonight, let's just enjoy how amazing this is. We found you, and you found us. There's a miracle in that. We'll tackle the rest as it comes."

She nodded and pulled my arm tighter around her. "It is, but will it be enough?"

I couldn't say anything more after that. What was there to say, except for... *I fucking hope so*. All of our intertwined futures depended on it.

CHAPTER 12

JASE

Waking up with my arm wrapped firmly around Tiffany's warm, naked body, was bliss. Her head rested on my chest and her hair tickled my nose. I opened my eyes and turned my head slowly, not wanting to wake her up. Judging from the loud snores around me, Fin and Ollie weren't awake yet either.

I stared at Tiffany for a long moment, drinking in the miracle of our mate. A few days ago, I'd been totally bummed about having to come home for Christmas and to our slowly dying pack.

I'd wanted to stay up in Ontario, happily ignoring the fact that we didn't have much of a future but choosing to accept that our present had been good enough.

We'd had a cheap place to stay, a little work, girls, and beer. It had been simple, and it certainly didn't make me jump for joy or anything, but it had been better than the depression I knew would be waiting for me when I got home. To my parents with no grandchildren. To the pack with no women.

Instead, this obligatory family trip had turned into the best thing that had ever happened to me. I'd found my mate, a person I was sure hadn't existed.

The boys and I had tried almost twenty packs, over ten states, and not one had a woman who held a candle to how I felt when I was near Tiffany. She made me feel like a man again. I was finally beginning to feel whole once more. Like my life had a purpose now.

And the fact she already owned a property despite being so young? That had blown me away. She was driven and fearless. We could all learn a lot from her, and in that way, I felt unworthy of her. But we would make it up to her. I was certain. I'd spend the rest of my life making sure that she was loved and taken care of. This was only the beginning of our lifetime together, after all.

"Mm, good morning," Tiffany said softly.

"Good morning," I said, trying to match how quiet she was being.

She still hadn't opened her eyes, but her dark eyelashes fanned out against her cheeks in a beautiful way.

"Damn, you're perfect," I said, tucking her long blonde hair behind her ear and letting my eyes trail down her neck to the swell of her perky breasts. If I'd been a photographer, there would be no way I'd be able to stay in bed and just stare at her. I would have wanted to jump up and grab my camera so I could capture the exquisiteness of my mate for all of time.

She opened her eyes and stared up at me, looking a little wary. "What do you mean?" she asked, pulling the sheet higher so her pink nipples disappeared from my view.

I tried not to be too disappointed that she was covering herself up. It wasn't like she was a super confident woman of the world. Not yet anyway. I grinned at her. "Well, let's start with your perfect face, your cute nose, and your stubborn chin." I kissed the tip of her nose, then her plump lips, just because I could; not because my cock was beginning to stir beneath the sheets now that she was awake.

"Yeah..."

"You're determined, courageous, and obviously stubborn," I said, then kissed her forehead and both cheeks this time.

She drew back to frown at me. "You know all this already, do you?"

"Absolutely."

"Anything else?" she asked, and the men on either side of us began to stir.

I reached under the covers, flipped her onto her back, and climbed on top of her possessively. "Yeah," I growled. "You're so hot I can't wait for you to have our babies."

Her eyes widened as her legs opened for me.

I didn't try to slide inside her just yet; I didn't trust her body not to be sore still from last night.

"You want to have kids soon, too?" she whispered.

I grinned. "Sweetheart, with you? Even today isn't too soon."

She turned her head toward Ollie. "Do you all feel that way?"

Ollie slid forward and kissed her lips, getting too close to me in that move. "Yeah. Of course."

I bumped forward, pressing my hard cock against Tiffany's pussy.

She flinched.

I withdrew straight away. "Tender?"

She nodded, sitting up, her pink-tipped breasts just calling out to be kissed. "Can we have a shower then head back to the pack? I'm really excited to see if our mating has changed anything back home."

"Yeah, of course," I said, sliding off the bed and standing, willing my cock to behave and go down. Even after being rejected so nicely, I was still more than enthusiastic for her.

Tiffany got up, eyeing my wayward appendage. "I suppose, if you like..." Worry filled her eyes.

There was no way I was going near her if she was feeling like that.

The other two guys were already tugging on their clothes already, anyway—we all silently agreed.

I reached out for her and pulled her close. "No. We'll wait until you want us again."

"Oh, it's not that I don't want you," she said, running her hands up my arms, while pressing her naked body into mine.

I shivered and forced myself to focus. "No. You're sore, and there's a lot going on today. Let's get dressed and head over to the pack." That was the absolute last thing I wanted to do, though.

She went up on her tiptoes and kissed me, the sweetness of her lips making me moan with a renewed hunger. "Thanks, Jase." She bounded over to her clothes and dressed.

Damn it. I wasn't prepared for how desperately I'd want my mate. I ran a hand down my face, then lumbered over to my own pile of clothes and pulled on my jeans and shirt from last night. "You looked pretty wiped out when you zipped in last night, Ollie," I said. "What happened there?"

Ollie shrugged. "Not sure. Bella said it's normal to feel shit when you first transport. Or get transported. Don't know what it's called."

Tiffany giggled from the corner. "It's called a transportational spell. And yeah, it affects shifters the most. Though I'm not sure why exactly. But I've been told its kind of like a bad travel sickness."

Ollie pulled on his work boots and grinned. "It was worth it to get to you last night. And I'd do it again."

I rolled my eyes. "You just wanted to make a dramatic entrance."

The guys laughed and together we made our way out of the motel and onto the street.

I filled my lungs with fresh air, breathing deep. The sun was warm on my face, the air crisp. It wasn't just a new day, but a new start to our life. I took Tiffany's hand and began walking toward our car. "Do you want to grab some breakfast, or..."

"I really want to just get to Ruby's. We can probably get some food at Milly's or something if you guys are hungry," she offered.

I opened the car door.

Tiffany jumped inside. She really was desperate to get home.

I slid into the driver's seat, a little disappointed that we couldn't spoil our girl with sex and breakfast in bed this morning.

Ollie and Fin climbed into the back of the car, ready to go.

I turned the key in the ignition. I needed to focus. Today wasn't about us. There was a lot more going on with Tiffany, and her family, and the pack.

"Do you go to Milly's a lot?" I asked, as we started the drive back to the pack.

Tiffany burst out laughing. "You could say I've practically *lived* there the past month or so."

"Why would you do that?" I asked. "The burgers are good and all. But..."

She bit her lip and glanced out the window. "You're going to think I'm crazy."

"Not likely," Fin said. "Tell us."

Tiffany sighed loud enough to be heard throughout the car. "I was the last one of my friends to find my soul mate, and since we all assumed that my mates would be from your pack as well, Jackson and Billy recommended I hang around Milly's since the pack *all* go in there. But sitting there by myself, day after day, just made me feel lonelier. And since I'm a witch, not many of the guys even wanted to chat with me, let alone look at me as being their possible mate, so..." She crossed her arms over her chest.

I reached across the car to grip her knee. "Of course, they didn't come over. They weren't your mates, gorgeous. And I'm sorry you had to wait so long for us to come home."

She turned to me and pouted prettily. "Yeah. You guys should have been here waiting for me. I would have found you so much earlier."

I smiled at her, then looked back at the road, turning into the pack's territory. "We're almost at Ruby's place, so hopefully you'll get some good news soon."

Tiffany slid to the edge of her seat. "Can you imagine if the spell has broken? We would be total heroes." She laughed to herself.

I glanced at the rearview mirror and at the two other guys. I didn't know anything, *literally* anything about curses, but I couldn't imagine them being broken easily. "Let's go see," I said as I pulled the car into a park on the opposite side of the street to where Jackson lived. "Looks like there's a few people here."

"Yeah," she said, pointing to a small blue mini. "That's my mom's car. And there's Ruby's mom. Looks like everyone's here." Tiff got out of the car, crossed the road, and rushed up to the front door.

We got out of the car more slowly.

A cold premonition rolled over me. There was no cheering coming from inside the house, and there was no happiness abounding in the streets. I would have assumed that if we'd broken the spell that had held our pack hostage for over twenty-two years, there would have been some sign of a celebration. "What do you think?" I asked Ollie and Fin. "Do you think anything will be different?"

Both guys looked at me, dread in their eyes.

"Nope," Ollie said, glancing down at the sidewalk and thrusting both hands into his pockets. "I think our mate is going to be sorely disappointed soon and we're going to have to deal with the fall out."

Tiffany glanced over her shoulder as she opened the front door, a huge grin on her face. She called out. "Come on, guys!" And ran into the house.

I groaned. "I know we're not warlocks or anything, but I've got a feeling this is going to be bad."

Fin shuddered. "Me too. And I don't want Tiffany to be upset, but she's going to be."

A soft cry came from inside the house.

My ears pricked up. "You guys hear that?"

Ollie groaned. "Yep. Shifter hearing sucks sometimes. Let's go."

I thrust my hands into my jeans pockets too and led the charge across the road and up to the front door. Someone was crying inside, and every part of me hurt to think it was our new mate.

CHAPTER 13

TIFFANY

Tears flowed down my face as I stared at my best friend lying on her death bed. Ruby was as pale as Snow White from the fairytale, but her lips weren't a ruby red, and her hair wasn't a raven black. Instead, my friend's normally lustrous red hair was limp, and carrot colored. Even her lips were pale.

"What's happened to her?" I sobbed, stumbling over to the bed. I slid onto the bed with her and reached for her hand. "I thought the stasis spell was going to help her stay in a stable condition!"

My mom put an arm around my shoulders. "It's meant to, honey. But unfortunately, as you can see, she's just getting worse, and a stasis spell is only ever temporary."

My throat burned with tears, and I swallowed hard to force the lump down so I could speak again. I'd been hoping, so much, that I would arrive at Ruby's to find her awake and healthy, and our father's human again. *Stupid, Tiffany. Stupid.* As if I was going to be central to breaking the spell.

Bella was sitting on the other side of the bed.

Ruby's mom hovered around the room.

"Our moms have done everything they can, Tiff," Bella said. "But it's possible we're going to have to..."

"No," I said, shaking my head. "*No.* You can't. We need more time."

Bella cleared her throat.

I turned around to face her.

"Have you mated with your triad?"

I nodded, another tear slipping unwanted down my cheek. *Traitor. I'm trying to be strong here.* "Yeah, I did. I was hoping it would help."

Bella smiled softly. "Yeah, so did I. Obviously our happiness isn't linked to breaking this curse, after all."

I wiped away the next tear that fell. "Only our deaths."

"Don't talk like that," Mom said. "We're not going to let anything happen to you. And we're going to save Ruby. There has to be a way."

"What about her baby?" I asked.

Jackson, who I hadn't noticed hanging around the back corner of the room, stood up and walked out. That answered my question.

My guys' voices came from the front of the house, and a wave of happiness spread through me. There *was* some good to focus on, but not here. Not today. Rather than railing against the inevitable, I chose to focus on what could be done. "So, what are our options?"

"Abort the pregnancy is probably the best one at this stage," my mom said. and

Ruby's mom sobbed. She covered her mouth and closed her eyes.

My heart went out to Sherie. I loved Ruby like a sister, but her mom must be in so much anguish over this decision. Not that we really had much of a choice it seemed. Lose one or lose them both.

"Okay," I said, nodding, taking it all in. "But what else?"

My mom sniffed, her eyes filled with sadness. "There isn't anything else."

"How long can you give us before you do anything?" I asked. *Forgive me, Ruby.*

Mom glanced over at Sherie. "About twenty-four hours. No more. After that, I don't think we'll be able to bring Ruby back at all."

That was another day. One more day. We had time. Then I realized we were missing someone. Bella's mom wasn't present. "Where's Kathy?"

"She's at the church, talking to some of the Coven members," Bella said. "We got a lead on where Tabitha had disappeared to, and Mom was just following up."

"What lead?"

"Her mom," Sherie said. "She still lives in town."

"Her mom?" I asked. "Why would that be important?"

"Oh! We didn't tell you," Bella said. "We found out that Tabitha was actually the daughter of the old High Warlock. He never married her mom, and it was all hush-hush when she was born... but that's why she's on the council. Or was. And why she's such a strong witch."

"You mean *bitch*," I corrected, flicking my hair over my shoulder, fire brewing inside me.

Bella chuckled.

Even Sherie gave me a half smile against her tears.

Mom tapped me on the shoulder.

I turned to give her my attention.

"But it also explains why she cursed you three last month and attacked Bella's mates."

I nodded. It was starting to make sense. They were right. "And why she hates wolf shifters so much."

"What do you mean?" Mom asked, tilting her head.

"She was *really* nasty to Ruby when we went to the church to ask them questions," I said. "She told her that she was a traitor. If her father hated wolf shifters so much that he cursed the whole pack, then he probably passed that prejudice onto her." Bigotry and hatred ran in families. Not the way blue eyes did, of course. It was taught. Handed down. It wasn't a coincidence.

"Do you really think the answer lies with the High Warlock and his daughter?" Bella asked.

I shrugged. "It looks like it might. The High Warlock told the pack Elders that he cursed them using our moms. Then Tabitha told us the spell was grounded with us. Which sucks by the way. Now we learn she's actually his daughter, so of course she knew about all that from the very beginning." The pieces of the puzzle were all clicking into place.

"But how the hell do we break the spell without dying?" I asked, more to myself.

According to Tabitha, us dying was the only way we were going to lift the spell. *But then she would say that, wouldn't she? She probably just wants us dead along with the wolves.*

"We could look into the past and see what they did. How they did it. See if the answer is there," Bella whispered fiercely, like we were holding a conspiracy meeting.

"Bella, *no*. You can't," my mom said flatly, like it was absolutely not an option.

"She can't, what?" I didn't understand. "And why would Bella do it?"

Bella stared at me. "Because the moms need to stay here and keep Ruby stable. They can't leave. But I can."

"It's dangerous to look into the past, Bella. You know you're not meant to," my mom said.

Sherie chewed on her bottom lip. She looked worried, but not enough to intervene, apparently—not when her own daughter's life was on the line.

Ollie stuck his head in and met my gaze "Are you okay, gorgeous?"

I waved my hand at him. It was obvious he didn't want to step into the room with all the witches and their emotions charging the space.

"Yeah, I'm okay. You guys catch up with Jackson and I'll be out in a bit."

He winked at me and smiled at Bella. "Thanks again for last night, Bella."

She lifted her chin and nodded like a teacher admonishing him. "I'm just glad you got your ass into gear and asked for help."

"Never too old to learn, I guess," he said. With that, he popped back out.

I glanced at Bella. "Thank you for helping him get to me last night."

Bella ran a hand through her hair. "It was nice to be asked, actually."

I didn't muse on the fact that Bella had bonded with one of my mates. I could feel the tiny barb of jealousy and tried hard to push it away. In the past, Bella wouldn't have even looked at a man. Now that she was bonded to three of them, she seemed more confident about, well, *everything*.

I shook myself. "Back to the past thing. I don't really understand what you want to do, and why it's so dangerous."

Bella watched Ruby before replying. "Scrying into the future or the past is frowned upon, but I've always been good at it."

"So, you can look into the past and see what they did to us? Really? Even back before we were born?"

Bella glanced at Sherie, then back at me. "Yeah, I can."

"It's dangerous, Bella!" Sherie said, clearly realizing how serious Bella was about endangering herself. "You don't understand! Your mind could get lost in the past, forever."

"We don't have any other choice," Bella said stiffly with determination. "What other solutions have you come up with?" Bella put both hands on her hips and held Sherie's eye.

Sherie finally collapsed on the bed and faced her daughter, caressing Ruby's cheek. "She wouldn't want you to put your life on the line, Bella. I know that much."

"I can do this," Bella said. "In fact, I think we should do it right now."

Sherie jumped to her feet. "We should wait for your mom, at least, please."

"There's no time," Bella said. "We need to work out what he did so we can undo it. That might take us the full day, maybe longer. We have to start as soon as possible." Bella grabbed my hand and tugged me toward the door to the bedroom. "Can you ask your mates to wait outside? I'll get set up in the dining room." She pulled me into the lounge.

My three gorgeous mates were all milling around the island in the kitchen.

Jackson was frying up eggs and bacon by the smell of it and toast was piling up.

"Maybe we can do it in the front room?" I asked.

The small lounge at the front of the house was more like a formal sitting room.

"Everything okay, gorgeous?" Ollie asked, turning around to look at me as he bit down on some buttery toast.

I nodded. "Bella's going try a spell that might help us find out where this curse came from in the first place."

His eyebrows climbed high on his forehead. "Cool. Need us for anything?"

I grinned at him. I loved that he offered, but what was a wolf shifter going to do to help with a scrying spell?

"Do you want some breakfast?" Ollie asked me, grabbing for a plate.

I shook my head. I was too nervous to eat. "I'll join you guys later."

"Come on," Bella said, and dragged me into the front room.

My mom appeared through the door as we settled on the ground.

Bella pulled her scrying crystal from her bag. "Got it with me this time," she said with a smile.

"You know, a séance would probably be more effective for this," Mom said as she kneeled down on the carpet on the other side of the coffee table. "Since the High Warlock passed away last year."

Bella arranged the crystal ball on the table and knelt in front of it, her attention zeroing in on the object. "I don't want to speak to the dead. I just want to know what happened that day." Bella closed her eyes as the purple magic began to swirl inside the orb.

"You didn't explain why this was so dangerous," I whispered to my mom.

"We don't know exactly why," Mom said, her gaze flicking from me to Bella, and back again. "We just know that looking into the past can be dangerous. Like Sherie said, we know a witch's consciousness can get lost…"

Bella gasped and took her hands off the orb. Her eyes flew open, and she stared at me, her expression wracked with shock. "Oh, my God. It wasn't him."

I frowned. "What do you mean? Who's he? And what didn't he do?"

"It wasn't the High Warlock," she said. "The spell he cast on us when our moms were pregnant was literally just to stop us from shifting. He didn't do anything else. He didn't harm us in any way beyond that."

I frowned at her. "That's impossible. You said that the wolf Elders admitted that the High Warlock told them that he, himself had cursed them."

Bella pressed her lips together. "Well, he was lying. Or someone else did the curse instead and he took the credit for it. Either way, it wasn't him."

I slumped. "But we need to find out who did it and how. Can you follow the curse back in time? Or follow Tabitha maybe? What's another way to find the solution?"

Bella straightened up, pulled a hair elastic from her wrist, and tied her long dark hair up in a messy bun on top of her head. She was getting her serious on. "I can try."

"Bella," my mom said, "I know you two are ignoring me, but I'll warn you again, this is *dangerous*."

Bella shrugged. "I don't care. We're running out of time, and I know Ruby would do the same for me."

This time when Bella focused on the crystal ball, I felt the energy in the room shift. Something cold, and evil, was here. "Um, Bella… I'm not sure about this…"

Too late. She was already in. The smoke was swirling inside the scrying crystal, but this time the magic wasn't purple. It had turned a strange, sickly, and murky green. Sweat dotted Bella's brow and then she began to shake.

Worry punched me in the stomach, making me sick, and I reached out for Bella.

"*No!* Don't touch her," Mom warned, her command like the crack of a whip.

My arm froze mid-air.

The front door slammed open a moment later.

"What is she doing?" Kathy cried as she ran in and kneeled beside her daughter.

Bella's forehead creased as she frowned, concentrating hard on the crystal ball in front of her. "The key isn't Tabitha..." she panted, grimacing as she searched deeper, further into the past for our answer. "It's... her *mom*."

I gasped. "Could her mom have cursed the wolves? Maybe the High Warlock told her about us, and she linked the spell to us as babies?"

Bella shook her head trying not to break her focus. "No, it's not that. There's more—" Bella threw her head back suddenly and gasped for air, her eyes wide.

"Bella, come back," I pleaded, resisting the urge to grab her hand. "You've done enough."

She shook her head, her eyelids fluttering uncontrollably as her mouth fell open.

I looked between Kathy and my mom, panic swelling in my chest. "What's wrong with her? Why isn't she breaking the connection?"

Kathy leaned forward, studying her daughter intently. "She's looking for an answer, perhaps one she shouldn't know. The reason we ban looking into the past is because we don't know what's there; or how it will affect the future, or the person doing the scrying. Bella is forcing herself well past her limits for Ruby and the baby."

"What can we do?" I asked, scrambling to my feet in frustration. My heart thundered in my chest, and I couldn't stop tugging on my hair. I wanted to save Ruby and the baby too, but none of us wanted Bella to sacrifice herself! "What can you see, Bella?" I asked in desperation.

"They want us... to die..." Bella gasped. Then she whimpered in a way that had me kneeling quickly next to her again, desperate to help.

I looked across the table at my mom. "What do I do?"

She shook her head. "We can't do anything, Tiffany. I told you it was too dangerous. Bella knew the risks. This was her choice."

I slammed my hand down on the coffee table in outrage. "At least Bella is trying to do something to help! You three have done nothing but want to end Ruby's pregnancy!" That wasn't entirely fair, I realized. And yelling at my mom wasn't going to help.

Bella began to scream, her eyes wild.

Tears ran down my face. I felt completely helpless.

Then Bella fell deathly silent and slumped toward me.

I caught her in my arms, fully expecting to be shocked with the power of her magic, but there was nothing. I glanced at the crystal ball. The murky green smoke had dissipated, but there was a crack in the glass. "What happened to her?" I asked, hoisting my friend up as best I could.

Kathy reached over and checked Bella's pulse.

I stared at Bella's mom, my mouth open as I awaited an answer. *No. It's not possible.* "Tell me she's not..."

"She's alive," Kathy said. "Barely. Let's get her up."

I shook my head, determined to be of some use in this God-awful situation. "I've got this." I uttered the same levitation spell that I'd used on Ruby and slowly lifted Bella up in the air. I walked her carefully toward the bed where my other friend slept.

"What the fuck?" Ollie said, jumping to his feet from where he sat on a kitchen stool.

"What happened to her?" Jackson demanded, racing around the island to come up next to where Bella floated through the air as though she was asleep like some fairy tale princess.

I didn't bother wiping the tears from my face. I needed both hands to hold onto the spell that was carrying my friend to the bedroom. "Bella tried to look into the past, to see who cursed us, but she went too far—we think. She's passed out." I looked up at Jackson pointedly, trying to silently communicate that this really wasn't good.

He paled and nodded, understanding flickering in his gaze. "I'll go find Elliot." He raced off without another word.

I continued to maintain the levitation spell to get Bella into Ruby's bedroom. "Can you pull back the blankets, please?" I asked Sherie, who was still there, sitting a silent vigil by her daughter's bedside.

Sherie jumped up to help and tugged back the covers. "What happened?"

I lowered Bella gently, resting her on the mattress, her head on the pillow. Then I let go of the spell and pulled the blankets up over her with care. "We don't know," I said without looking at her. "She went searching for answers, and she hasn't come back again."

Sherie hurried over to the other moms, their frantic whispers filling the air around me.

But I couldn't drag my gaze from my two best friends. The sisters of my heart. My blood cousins.

Ruby was my fierce friend. She was the outspoken one. Eternally stubborn and great at magic. Bella, meanwhile, was my smart friend. She was good at everything, except speaking in large crowds. She was the most powerful of us all and she made me so grateful to be her friend.

Another tear ran down my face and this time I grabbed a tissue from the bedside table and wiped it away. "What are we going to do?" I asked the moms as I turned around to look at them.

They turned to face me.

All three of them seemed as lost as I felt. And despite the twenty-five years of life experience they had on me, I felt like I was the one who was older and wiser and more in control. "We have to do something," I said, "but what?"

My mum bit her lip. "All I can think is that we've already lost two of you and we can't lose you as well, Tiffany."

"Why would you lose me as well?" I asked. Then it came to me like a bright flash of lightning—an idea. "What if you put me into some sort of deathlike state?" I asked.

"What do you mean?" Mom countered, swallowing hard.

"I mean that the curse is linked to all three of us and our lives, and according to you, both Bella and Ruby are already as close to death as you can get. If you guys use magic to put me under as well, maybe we could trick the curse long enough for it to break!"

"That's crazy," Mom said, shaking her head.

"It may be," I replied with a smile, "but if it works then we might be able to save everyone and we won't have to die to do it."

The moms looked at each other, and there was finally a flare of hope glimmering through their fear.

I used that to my advantage. "Don't you all want our fathers back in human form? Don't you want to spend the rest of your lives loving the men that you should've had by your sides for the last twenty-three years? Don't you want to take back the lives that were stolen from you?"

Sherie looked at my mom, then at Kathy.

They were thinking about it.

"Could it really work?" Sherie asked.

Kathy tapped her lips as though she were reasoning out the logistics of it all. "I suppose... if it's true that the girls' lives are linked to the curse... But to do it, we'd actually need to stop their hearts. All at the same time. It'd be the only sure way to really fool the spell into accepting they were all gone."

I swallowed hard, the lump in my throat threatening to constrict my speech. "Could you do it?" I pressed. "Without really killing us, preferably?"

"If we did it as one, we could hold them that way for... what's safe?" Mom asked.

"Sixty seconds at the very most," Kathy said firmly.

Sherie nodded. "Sixty seconds should be safe enough, for Ruby's baby as well. If we tilt them all upside down the blood will rush closer to their hearts and brains."

My heart began to pound with fear. They were really going to do it. They were going to stop our hearts so that technically, we would all be 'dead'. "Okay, how do we do this then?" I asked, my voice breaking with stress.

My mom turned toward me. "We don't know if it will work, Tiff. Not for certain. Perhaps it's not worth the risk."

"Of course, it is!" I blazed. "You're three talented and powerful witches. Surely you can do something. What would you need?"

Mom turned to Kathy. "What do you think, Kath?"

Kathy walked to the head of the bed and put her hand out to feel Bella's cheek. "I think we need to do *something*. And it might be our best bet. This is only getting worse and worse. We almost lost them all to Tabitha's spell last month and now... this?" She sighed. "We need anchors."

"Anchors?" I repeated.

"Yes," Kathy said, spinning toward me. "The three of us can conduct the spell, but it would be safer if you three had another person to hold onto you during the minute you're gone. Someone to pull you back—someone you love."

"Our mates!" I cried. "Just one? Or would all three be better?"

Our moms exchanged glances.

"Traditionally, one lover would be enough. But since the three of you have three men each, I don't see why more would be a bad thing," Sherie said.

"It may even be enough to bring Bella back to us," Kathy said. "I can tweak the spell to pull Bella back up to consciousness as they rise."

"I can do the same for Ruby," Sherie said, "if we decide we want them all awake." A tear slid down her face.

It was in that moment I realized that our moms had planned on aborting Ruby's baby while she was still in a magical coma.

"Bring us all back," I demanded in a tone that challenged any opposition. *Ruby has the right to be a part of the decision.* Even if I knew deep down what she would likely choose. "If you can," I added.

"If we can," Mom repeated.

I tapped my fingers on the end of the bed, noticing for the first time just how big the damn thing was. There was about ten feet between Ruby and Bella. *I've got to get one of these when all this mess is sorted out.* Last night worked well pretty with the two king beds pushed together, but this would be better. I shook myself to clear my mind. "So, what's the next step? Gather all our mates?"

"Yes," Sherie said. "Meanwhile, we need to go home and collect some specific herbs for the incantation."

Kathy nodded, frowning in thought. "I need to get a book from my house too. And my wand."

My eyebrows climbed up my forehead. We didn't use wands much, almost at all, really. We were taught from a young age to do magic without them. But from what Bella had told me in the past, it would magnify a witch's power when necessity called for it.

"So, what?" I asked. "Meet back here in... an hour?"

It would take our moms half an hour to drive to town and back.

Sherie shook her head. "No. Make it fifteen minutes. We'll travel the quick way. We don't have the time to waste."

The three moms stood together, shared a look, clicked their fingers, and they were gone.

I swayed on my feet, a wave of exhaustion making me close my eyes and reach for the foot board.

We'd been running for too long. Since before we were born our fathers had been cursed, and with that spell, it had cursed our whole lives; us girls to be fatherless and our mothers to be husbandless. It was time for it all to end. No matter what price we had to pay. No matter what I had to do. There had to be an end in sight.

I walked out the door the old-fashioned way and went about explaining to my mates what I was about to do.

Elliot the Alpha tore into the house looking for Bella like a bull in a China shop. Jackson had obviously successfully conveyed the seriousness of our situation.

I sighed. It was time to tell nine of the most possessive, strong, paranormal men that their mates were about to die... And that they had to hold us while our hearts stopped.

Lucky me.

"Sorry, what?" There was *no way* I just heard my mate correctly. "Ah, no. You're not fucking doing that!"

"I have to. We all have to," Tiff said, impassioned.

I shook my head and growled in frustration, crossing my arms over my chest to stop myself from reaching for her. Why wasn't anyone else telling her she was crazy? Surely the other guys felt the same way I did?

"You want to... die?" Fin asked, his tone showing he was as clearly as baffled as I was.

"Hell no!" She glared at him in indignation. "How can you even think that?"

All three of us, her mates, relaxed into the couch a little easier upon hearing that.

"But that doesn't mean I don't have to do it," she added quietly.

I groaned and sat up straighter. *Great*, all that tension was back. "I... don't get it," I said, then glanced around the room at the other guys.

Tiffany had sent Jackson and Elliot out to find the others, and within ten minutes, all nine of us witch mates were crammed into the lounge together. Three Alphas. Five Betas. And a warlock-wolf just for something different. We made for a pretty impressive unit, and in a way, I felt lucky to be included in such an elite group.

"Explain it to me again," Elliot said, his voice rough with emotion. "What happened to Bella?"

Tiffany swallowed hard.

I reached for her hand, gripping it to offer my support.

Elliot was by far the most intimidating of us all, and although I could tell he was trying hard to control his anger, it was still currently directed at Tiffany—*my* mate.

"Um..."

There was a glimmer of light, then suddenly three older ladies materialized into the kitchen, chattering away like birds.

"Oh," one of them said.

Then all three turned to look at us.

The one on the left, who had dark hair, grinned. "That is *a lot* of men." Tiffany's mom put a hand over her mouth, I think to stop the laugh from exploding through. Now really wasn't the time to laugh.

To be fair, though, from her perspective, *yeah*, there were a lot of guys in this room and a shit load of testosterone.

Elliot stood up.

I stared up at him. *Damn,* he was tall.

"Kathy. What happened to Bella?" he asked, unsatisfied with Tiff's slow start.

Bella's mom stepped forward, putting a trembling hand on the marble kitchen counter that stood between the women and us. "I don't know for sure," she answered. "But she was doing a spell that allowed her to look into the past. And when she did, she seems to have gotten lost somehow. The magic that it required was too much for her to take. We rarely delve into the past for exactly this reason."

Bella's other mates stood up.

"What can we do?" they asked in unison.

I stood up as well. "We don't want Tiffany risking herself."

Tiff glared at me.

"But we'll do anything to help you fix this," I added quickly.

"Good," Tiffany's mom said, stepping forward. "We're going to need all nine of you to make sure we get our daughters back."

"Explain that to me." Fin said, coming to stand next to me.

"Basically," Kathy began, "we need all nine of you to hold your mates in your arms, so that when we re-start their hearts and bring them back to us, they have an anchor to hold onto. Something worth returning for. The journey back isn't always easy."

"We'd do it," Tiffany's mom interrupted, glancing at her witch friends, "but the spell itself is going to need all of our combined magic and power, so we need to be able to focus on that."

"If you need a timekeeper," Jase said, "I'm freakishly good at measuring time. I can tell you exactly when sixty seconds is up."

Tiffany's mom smiled gently at him. "We'll use someone's phone and alarm just to be sure, but... there is a possibility... if something goes wrong with us, or the spell, or the electronics in the room, then yes. Keep count of the sixty seconds they're going under for, just to be safe. Please."

Jase was weirdly good at telling the time. He never wore a watch, and yet he still always knew what the time was, right down to the minute. Or how long had lapsed from one event to another.

Jackson clapped his hands together. "All right, how are we doing this?"

"Let's go into the bedroom," Kathy advised, and she began arranging people.

Ruby's mates all got on the massive bed to take her in their arms.

"Make sure her feet are raised above her head. The blood needs to stay in their brains and hearts as long as possible, so hopefully they won't even realize their hearts stopped beating for a whole minute," said Kathy.

I held Tiffany's hand in mine and dragged her closer to me. "We only just found you. You are not allowed to die on us. Do you hear me?" I whispered in her ear. I understood that this spell was purely a ploy, a trick, of sorts to break the curse. But Tiffany's heart *really* was going to stop beating and it was obvious from the fear I could scent in the room, that there was a real danger here of things going terribly wrong.

Tiffany turned her head.

Our gazes connected, clashing with the heat and passion of two stubborn people in love.

I swallowed hard as the realization hit me. I loved this woman already. *Now I really can't lose her.*

Tiffany pressed her lips to mine, kissing me like a woman drowning, searching for the air within me.

I kissed her with every pent-up emotion inside of me. I held nothing back as my tongue swept inside her mouth and my hands squeezed her body tight to me.

Then, too soon, she pulled away from me, smiling up at me with tears in her eyes. "I'm not going anywhere. But what you three need to understand, is that these two girls are the closest things I've ever had to sisters. They're my cousins by blood, but they've been my whole entire world since we were kids. Nothing can stop me from helping them."

"Then we're here for you, whatever you need," Jase said, stepping up and tugging Tiff into him.

I glanced at the bed, where Bella's mates had picked her up and now held her in their arms.

Ruby's mates had done the same.

"It's your turn, Tiff," Tiffany's mom said as she touched her daughter gently on the arm.

Tiff inhaled sharply, then nodded. "Let's do this." She climbed onto the end of the massive bed.

I took a moment to assess the size of it. "Whoa, is this like... custom made?"

Jackson glanced over at me, where he sat at the other end holding Ruby's head. "Yeah."

He didn't expand further, so I made a mental note to ask about it later—when all this was over.

Jase and Fin sat down.

Tiffany lay over them.

I climbed on too.

She stretched her legs over me. "You'll need to hold my legs up once the spell is going," Tiffany said to me, her eyes wide with barely restrained fright.

I nodded. *She's so brave.* "Not a problem, babe. I've got you."

"We're ready to start," Bella's mom said.

The moms walked around the room and stood at each end of the bed.

One on the left, one on the right, one at the end near us.

A triangle of power.

Three daughters. Three mothers. Three mates for Ruby, Bella, and Tiffany.

Strange pattern, really.

"It's important than none of you freak out, run out, or attempt to touch us, okay?" Bella's mom said as she tossed some sort of smelly powder in the air. She spoke some strange words, then using her magic, she made the powder hover over the three girls and sprinkle down over them.

Tiffany lay back and didn't say anything. She closed her eyes and began to breathe deeply.

"Why would we do that?" Fin asked.

Kathy's lips trembled into a weary smile. "Because it's about to get intense in here. We're trying to break a twenty-three-year-old curse and none of us have done this spell before. Instructions still hold. No matter what, do not let go of your mates. You are their literal anchor in this world, gentlemen, and without you, we might all lose them forever."

My heart squeezed tight at the thought of losing Tiffany for even a minute, let alone forever.

Kathy narrowed her eyes and glared at me. "And *do not* leave that bed."

I nodded once. *I got it.*

The three protective moms moved into their final positions.

Kathy pulled out a wand from one of the pockets hidden within the long folds of her skirts.

My mouth dropped open. "Whoa." *A fucking wand!*

"Concentrate!" Fin snarled, whacking me in the chest.

I growled at him and gripped Tiffany's legs tighter. "I am, but this is some freaky shit!"

All three moms began to speak in a language I didn't understand. Smoke soon filled the room, beginning at carpet level then rising up, like we were in some sort of band with special effects on stage or something.

"Who turned on the smoke machine?" I mumbled under my breath.

There was a loud growl from the other side of the bed.

I took that as a sign that I needed to shut the fuck up. It sounded like Elliot, or one of the other Alphas.

Tiffany began to gasp and struggle against us.

"Hold her," Jase said.

All three of us clung tighter to our mate as she kicked and moaned in pain.

The mom's voices grew higher, and louder.

Tiffany screamed.

I swore under my breath and held tight to my mate. The sound unnerved my very soul. Every instinct in me raged to protect her, but there was nothing I could do but follow the witches' instructions. *This is getting seriously intense.*

Tiffany stopped, sagging over us. Then she stopped breathing.

"Lift her legs!" someone yelled from across the smoke-filled bedroom.

I jumped, then grabbed hold of Tiffany's ankles and lifted them high in the air.

She was still. And cold. And pale.

I shook from the stress of it all and time seemed to cease holding any meaning.

"Oh, my God. Oh, my God," Jase was saying beside me. "That's thirty seconds."

My wolf howled inside my mind and I began to shiver. *No. No!* I would not shift. I would not abandon my mate or ruin this spell. There was too much at stake!

The moms' continued chanting.

"That's fifty seconds!" Jase yelled out, a bit louder this time.

White light suddenly erupted from the center of the bed and exploded through the room. The aftershock swept through all of us, humming with magical electricity. Wind kicked up around the room, and the curtains flapped so hard that the curtain rod twisted free.

My vision was obscured by the strength of the wind in my face. I lifted Tiffany's legs higher, until her butt was up in the air as well out of sheer panic.

"That's sixty seconds!" Jase yelled at the top of his lungs over the roar of wind that filled the room. "Stop!"

The moms ceased chanting. Then, as one, they collapsed to the ground.

The wind died, the smoke evaporated as though it had never been, and an unsettling stillness descended.

Next to me, Tiffany's mom lay in a heap on the floor. Her eyes were closed and her mouth was open as though she were panting for breath and utterly exhausted.

"Is she alive?" I asked to no one in particular. "Quick, check her breathing!"

Fin reached out and pressed his fingers against Tiffany's neck.

"Fuck, what have we done?" he said.

My heart pounded even harder than it already had been.

Jackson called out to his Beta. "Look, I can see her breathing, check her pulse. Quick Billy."

There was a frantic rush to check all three mates for their breathing, their heartbeat, any signs of life.

All the moms were still passed out and hadn't moved. Considering the sort of spell they'd just conducted, literally draining the life and taking the heartbeat from their daughters, I could only imagine how much effort and strength all three of the older witches had to exert to maintain control.

"Hang on, wait, look!" Jase said.

I stared at Tiffany's face. Her color began to return. The paleness that had haunted her cheeks disappeared and the pinkness came back. Then her perky, gorgeous breasts began to rise and fall with each breath she took.

She opened her eyes and looked up at us.

The tangible sense of relief that washed over me made me weak.

"Did it work?" she whispered, her voice hoarse.

CHAPTER 16

TIFFANY

I feel like I've been hit by a truck. My skin was clammy, my heart was pounding, and there was an overall fatigue throughout my whole body that was stifling. I felt completely drained of energy. And when I opened my eyes, I was still lying on my back with my legs in the air, fully clothed and surrounded by all three of my mates.

"Well?" I asked them, looking between each of their intense sets of eyes. "Did it work?"

Jase ran a hand over my forehead and down my cheek. "How do we know if it worked or not?" he lovingly asked.

I sighed. "Help me up, please." I reached for Jase and Fin.

They grabbed an arm each and slowly pulled me back up again.

Meanwhile, Ollie gently let my legs go.

Soon I was sitting upright on Ruby's bed, my head spinning. I turned around and glanced at my two best friends who were still being held by their mates. "How are they?" I asked. "Is Ruby okay? Is Bella all right?" I scoured their forms for signs of life. My heart was in my throat and my stomach was twisting with anxiety, but I counted my heartbeats... one, two, three. I held my breath.

Just as I was about to resign myself to the fact that my friends weren't going to wake, Bella's eyes fluttered open.

She sat up between her mates and put a hand to her head. "What happened?"

"Your scrying spell knocked you out," I said. "You put in too much power or something."

Bella shook her head at me. "No, it wasn't that. It was something in the past. Something in that group of witches and warlocks. I couldn't get out of there without the right information."

"What did you learn?" I asked. "Can you remember anything now?"

"Don't worry about any of that now," Tommy said evenly.

"You're alive," Elliot said. "That's all that matters."

Bella smiled at them but then she looked at me and said, "I have a few things to tell both of you."

I gazed over at Jackson who was still holding Ruby. "Is she awake?"

"I don't know," Jackson answered. "I think she's alive. Her heart is beating but she isn't waking up."

"Hang on, wait a second," Darren said. "Her eyelids are moving! I think she's waking up."

Excitement flashed through me, and I couldn't contain my smile as Ruby opened her eyes for the first time in days.

She looked from one person to another. "What's happened? What's everyone doing here?" Then she giggled. "And why is everyone in our bedroom?"

I scrambled across the bed as I laughed and dragged her into my arms, hugging her close while pushing her big mates out of the way. "I can't believe you're alive," I said, then pulled back and gazed at her. "How are you feeling?"

Ruby stared at me as though she didn't understand the question. "I'm okay, I suppose. How are you?"

I laughed out loud at her casual response. I couldn't help myself. It seemed simply amazing to me that she was sitting there looking at me and talking to me as though nothing was wrong—when half an hour ago we were concerned she wouldn't even make it through the day.

A sudden thought hit me and I jumped, sliding off the bed with excitement. "We need to go check and see if our dads are still in wolf form." I glanced down at Sherie, who was still lying on the floor. I kneeled beside her and put my fingers to her neck, checking for a pulse, to see if her heart was still beating. She seemed all right, so I told Ruby to see if she could do anything to get the moms to wake up.

I bolted out the door and into the backyard and stopped dead on the patio.

The three gray wolves, still in animal form, lounged on the grass.

I stumbled forward with so many mixed emotions pulsing through me that I couldn't stand. I pushed my hands against the wood of the railing as I stared at the wolves. It didn't work. There's no way it worked, if our dads were still in wolf form.

There was the sound of steps behind me and a hand slid across my shoulder. "Does this mean the spell tonight didn't work?" It was Ollie.

I looked up at him. "I don't think so. But it was worth a try."

I certainly had no regrets. We'd gotten Ruby back at least. But if the pack and our dads were part of the same spell, then the three of us being dead for one minute hadn't broken the curse.

Ollie kissed me gently and then led me back inside to the kitchen area for a glass of water. Within a few minutes, the room was full of people and this time Bella and Ruby were on their feet. The moms were up and about too, milling around and checking on everyone.

Someone's phone rang and Elliot reached for his cell. "Hey Dad, I'm just a little busy with something, can I call you—" he stopped, and then said, "No way! Seriously? I can't believe it." He turned to stare at me, his eyes wide. Something had happened. "Yeah, yeah, I'll tell them," Elliot said, then hung up the phone.

"What was it?" Tommy asked.

"You won't believe it," Elliott said, "but Cynthia gave birth today."

"Cynthia, as in Nathaniel's mate?" Tommy said.

"Yeah." Elliot grinned. "They thought they were having a boy... like we always do. But... she just had a little girl!"

"Bullshit," Tommy said.

Elliot laughed, his deep chuckle rolling through the room. "Yeah, that's kind of what I was thinking, but my dad would never bullshit about something like that."

Ruby's face lit up, her hand moving to her belly. "Does that mean we *did* break the spell? Could we have broken the curse on the pack?"

"But the dads are still wolves," I said. "We didn't break the curse."

Bella turned to me. "Unless the spell on our dads and the curse on the pack was done by two people, not one. They would have had to link each spell to two different things. If the pack's curse is linked to us, then by dying metaphorically and physically for a single minute, we've broken that curse. But if our dads' inability to return to human form was done by another witch or a warlock, then we need to find out the link to that."

I stared at her "You said you had to talk to Ruby and me about something you saw when you were scrying," I prompted.

Bella nodded slowly. "Yeah, I do, and it's starting to make more sense now that I know that the dads and the pack were affected by two different spells."

Our mates and the pack members started to chat happily over their cells, talking about the prospect of the curse finally being broken. It meant daughters for the pack. It meant mates for the sons of their friends.

I went over to Ruby and held her hand. "Do you think we can go and talk now?"

Although I was relieved that the pack's curse was finally broken, assuming the birth of the first daughter in twenty-three years proved that it had been, I was worried about the fact that our fathers were still in wolf form.

The moms stayed in the kitchen to prepare food. They were looking pale, but relieved.

Bella glanced that way and said, "Yeah, Ruby, is there anywhere we can go and have a quick chat about what I saw?"

Ruby nodded. "Let's go upstairs to one of the spare bedrooms, and let these guys celebrate the fact that the pack now has a future." Her hand slipped down to cover her stomach once more. "And hopefully, so do I…" A smile rippled on her lips, and I knew deep down that some part of her knew that she almost lost her life and that of her baby.

Ruby walked toward the stairs and called out to Jackson that she was just heading upstairs with us for ten minutes and would be back soon.

The three of us went up the stairs and into a bedroom with a nice queen-sized bed.

Ruby shut the door behind us. "Sit on the bed if you like," she said.

Ruby and I ended up sitting on the bed and faced Bella.

She paced up and down the bedroom.

"What did you see, Bella? Can you remember?" I asked.

"Yes. I remember everything. But before we move on, I need to say thank you. I know that you put yourself in harm's way for us."

Ruby glanced from Bella to me, and back again. "What did I miss?"

I laughed. "Only the fact that the curse on the pack almost killed you and your baby. The only way to save you was to try and get rid of the pregnancy, and even then the moms weren't sure that you would survive the process."

Ruby gasped, blatant surprise and pain on her face. Then she slid her hand down to hold her pregnant stomach. "They wouldn't…"

Bella smiled gently at her. "They would have, and almost did. Your mates and the moms would have done anything to save you, Ruby. I must admit that I was willing to do anything to save you, too." Tears slipped down her cheeks. "I'm so sorry."

Ruby nodded slowly. "I understand. I suppose if the roles were reversed, I would've done the same thing for either of you."

Bella smiled sadly again. "Well, Tiffany wouldn't have. She fought to save you and the baby. Elliot told me that it was her idea to get them to kill her, as well as us temporarily, to try and break the curse."

Ruby turned to me and smiled, tears in her eyes and glistening on her eyelashes. "Really? You fought for me and my baby?"

"Of course, I did," I said. "You're like a sister to me. Even more so."

"Thank you, Tiffany. I don't know how to thank you for saving me and my daughter. I think I would've been completely heartbroken if I'd woken up and she was gone."

I reached out and held Ruby's hands where they were lying in her lap. "I couldn't let them do what they wanted to do, even though I knew that their intentions were all good and they just wanted to save you."

"You did the right thing, obviously," Ruby said. "We broke the curse."

"We have one more thing to do," Bella said. "We need to break the curse on our dads, so we can finally have our families back together again."

"Who is it linked to?" Ruby asked.

"What do you mean, *who* is it linked to?" I asked.

Bella turned to me. "A spell this strong needs to be grounded in *someone*. It wasn't the High Warlock who did it though. He didn't do this side spell. It was someone who hates the wolves just as much as he did."

"Who was it, Bella?" Ruby asked, clutching her belly protectively.

I wanted to know the answer to the same question.

CHAPTER 17
TIFFANY

"Come on, Bella, please tell us." The need to know who we had to find and sort out was eating away at me. If it was one of the witches from the Coven, then we could handle that. If it was Tabitha? We might have more of a problem. No-one had seen her since she cursed us a month ago...

Bella crossed her arms over her chest and bit her lip, her expression one of anxiety.

Ruby jumped to her feet. "Come on! Tell us, Bella. *Please.*"

Bella huffed out a big sigh. "I'm not sure what we're going to do about it. It was Tabitha's mother. She's the one who hates the wolves just as much as the old High Warlock did."

My mouth dropped open. *Is she serious?* The bad guy that we were chasing was some... what? Seventy-year-old witch?

"Seriously?" Ruby said, voicing my thoughts aloud. "What does she have against the pack?"

Bella shook her head sadly. "From what I could see while I was looking back into the past, there was a reason the High Warlock never married. He was in love with a woman who was the Fated Mate to one of the wolves in the pack, which meant that rather than marrying the

High Warlock which she was destined to do according to our laws, she ran off and married the wolf shifter instead." She smiled suddenly, which surprised me.

What was funny about the situation?

Then she continued. "I'm pretty sure she was my grandmother, and Darren's as well."

Ruby chuckled at that too. "Darren will be *rapt* to hear that. He loves stories about our family."

I got to my feet since Ruby and Bella were now standing in the middle of the bedroom; I felt silly being the only one still sitting on the bed. "I'm sorry, I don't quite get why this is a big deal?" I couldn't work out the connection between Tabitha and our dads. *Sure, they were wolf shifters, but still...?*

Bella turned to me. "The High Warlock never married anyone. He went to his grave as an unmarried man still mourning the loss of the one woman he loved."

That didn't make sense. "But he had a daughter. Tabitha." I interjected. Had I missed something?

Bella smiled but it failed to reach her eyes. She still looked sad. "Yes, he did. That's the problem. He never married anyone because he could never love anyone but my grandmother. The woman who left him. But he sired a child with another woman, and I believe that Tabitha's mother loved him very much. She expected him to marry her and have more children and a life with her. But he never did."

"Why would he do that, though?" Ruby asked. "Because he couldn't get over your grandmother leaving him?"

"Probably," Bella said. "From what I saw, Tabitha's mother grew insanely jealous of my grandmother because of how the High Warlock loved her. So, she was left as a single mother raising a daughter, still living in the same town, within the same Coven, as a man that she loved, but who wouldn't marry her. And with that envy grew a hatred for the pack that only soured and continued to get worse over time."

"So, who did the curse that linked us to the pack?" I asked. "Was it

Tabitha or the High Warlock?" I was getting confused about who'd done what. *God, hate convolutes so much!*

"I believe that Tabitha's mother did both spells," Bella said finally. "The spell that was grounded in us and was linked to the pack's 'infertility'. But she also did another spell to punish our fathers for daring to impregnate our mothers, powerful witches, when they had no right to —according to her. And I believe she grounded that spell in her own daughter, to ensure our mothers and fathers suffered as long as she did."

Ruby and I gasped in union.

I put a hand over my mouth. *No way.*

"She wouldn't do such a thing, surely?" Ruby said.

"I think she did," Bella answered. "It would make sense if she wanted our fathers punished as long as possible. Her daughter is about ten years older than us and will live a lot longer than her mother will. And as we already know, when the individual that the spell is grounded in dies, then the spell breaks."

I couldn't believe that a mother would use her own daughter to ground a spell born of such hatred. *Surely that could cause long term effects?* "So, does that mean we need to find Tabitha and..." I didn't want to have to voice aloud that we needed to kill her, which it seemed we obviously did. So, I decided on a slightly more tactful route. "Does that mean we need to find a way of unlinking the grounding, then? Because I'm not leaving our dads in wolf form forever. I want my dad back."

Bella and Ruby stared at me, neither speaking.

I'd stunned them. *Great.* I bit my lip, forcing the tears I felt burning in my eyes to retreat. "I've never said that out loud before, but I do. I can't believe that for so many years I thought they'd abandoned us and our moms. Imagine what it would've been like for them! To have to leave their pack and everything they'd ever known. *To leave us.* To miss out on everything they could've had in their life, all because some stupid witch decided that they'd overstepped some ridiculous personal mortality line." I wiped away the hot tears that fell on my cheeks and swallowed hard. It was all so unfair.

Bella nodded. "You're right. It sucks on such a major level and yes, to answer your question. We need to find Tabitha and we need to work out if there's any way of unlinking the grounding—other than death."

We all knew the answer to that. We'd spent a month researching the topic and hadn't found one single good answer.

"We can always ask our moms to do the heart stopping spell on Tabitha as well, maybe?" I said. "We did it. We survived. And it worked." I was willing to do anything to have my dad in my life.

"So, what are we going to do?" Ruby asked.

"We need to find Tabitha," Bella said, "but I think the key is going to be to find her mother."

That sounded ominous. Were we going to use her mom as bait? Or could we put some sort of spell on her mother that would attract Tabitha to come back to town? Assuming she'd left.

"Do you think we need to ask our mates for help?" I asked. I was pretty sure the wolves were going to want to help us out, but I was also a little worried that they wouldn't stop at a heart-stopping spell once they got their hands on the woman who had tried to kill us a month ago.

"I think Elliot would probably kill her if he found her," Bella said.

She looked truly worried at the prospect. Elliot was an Alpha's alpha, one of the strongest and largest men of the pack. He was also known for being uncontrollable and for having an almighty temper on him.

Bella seemed to be able to control him extremely well but if he came across the woman who had tried to kill his mate, and had almost succeeded, would he be able to control his wolf long enough to leave Tabitha unharmed?

Though that would unhook our dads from the spell.

"Well, we need to do something," Ruby said. "I don't know what it is, but I feel like we're running out of time."

"At least we've severed the link to the curse on the pack," Bella said. "That's huge."

Bella was right. What we had achieved today was nothing short of incredible. We'd saved the pack from literal extinction, and we'd saved Ruby and her daughter as well.

Was it selfish to feel like we were losing the battle when my father was still lying in the sun outside in the backyard in his animal form?

He should be inside chatting with my mom about what we were going to do, enjoying a coffee or a homemade cookie. I didn't know what dads did, and I didn't really care, as long as I finally got to have one.

There was a knock on the spare bedroom door.

"Can we come in?" my mom called out hesitantly.

I walked over and opened the door with a smile. "Yeah, of course."

My mom rushed in and hugged me tightly.

I didn't question her sudden need for affection. I just hugged her tightly back. Over Mom's shoulder, I watched Kathy and Sherie do the same with their daughters, each holding Ruby and Bella in a firm embrace.

Ruby hugged her mom, before pulling back and glaring at her. "I can't believe you were going to abort my baby!"

A stab of guilt hit me. *I probably shouldn't have told her that.*

Sherie sighed and nodded. "To my shame, yes, to save you I would have."

Ruby's eyes welled up with tears, but just when I thought she might scream, or lash out at her mom in anger, she nodded in understanding and wiped the tears away that fell on her cheeks. "I guess I'm lucky that I had Tiffany there fighting for me and my little one."

All five women turned to me and stared.

I shook my head as heat flushed up my cheeks. "You would have done the same for me."

Ruby smiled.

I felt a swell of love in the room stronger than anything I'd ever felt before.

"Maybe, maybe not," Ruby said, shaking her head. "We'll never know. But you're amazing, Tiff. I know you don't see it sometimes, but you're *so* strong. And I really admire you."

I had to look away. My nose was tingling, and my throat was thick with emotion. I'd always felt inferior to my friend. Less nice. Less smart. Less beautiful. "I suppose being the most stubborn has its benefits," I offered.

Ruby crossed the room and hugged me. "It does when it comes with a heart of gold. Thank you again, Tiff."

I nodded and closed my eyes, so I didn't embarrass myself again.

"So, you three saved the day?" Sherie said, coughing to clear her throat. "The pack is finally free."

I pulled away from Ruby. "Well, it was you three who performed the spell," I said to our moms. "Your power and talent saved the pack. But we saved Ruby, too, and that's the best part for me."

Kathy turned to her daughter, her face suddenly somber. "Is there something you need to share with us?"

Bella nodded with a grimace. "I saw more than I was meant to while I was scrying into the past."

"And what did you find out?" my mom asked, her brows downturned heavily.

Bella sighed. "Basically, that the High Warlock didn't conduct any of the spells. It was his girlfriend, or lover, or whatever you want to call her."

"Eloisa?" Mom said, sounding surprised.

"Is that Tabitha's mom?" I asked. "Because she's apparently the key to it all."

Mom turned to me, her eyes wide and strangely frightened. "Yes. Eloisa is Tabitha's mother... and the old High Warlock's half-sister."

CHAPTER 18

TIFFANY

"What? No way!" My mouth dropped open. "Surely, that can't be right?"

Bella stepped forward. "You don't really mean that the High Warlock had a child with his *own* half-sister? I must have misheard you."

If Bella had misheard it, so had I, because that was exactly what it sounded like Mom said.

Sherie pressed her fingers into her temples as though she had a migraine building, then she nodded. "You heard correctly, all right. It's the greatest secret, and shame, of our Coven."

My mouth gaped wide like a fish.

Ruby put both hands up as though she was saying 'hold on'. "Are you telling me that Tabitha is the product of a half-brother-and-sister coupling?"

Our moms nodded.

I snorted. "No wonder she's so fucked up."

"Tiffany!" My mom admonished me.

"What? It's true!" I glared back at her.

Mom's mouth twisted as though she was trying not to laugh.

How screwed up must that poor woman be? Both genetically and mentally? I wondered.

"How did something like that even happen?" Bella spluttered.

Sherie ran a hand through her hair. "Well, we're not a hundred percent sure."

"Some people say she was the one to cast a love spell on him," Kathy whispered.

"And some say he didn't realize she was his half-sister until it was too late," my mom added.

I stared at the moms, aghast. "Seriously? How did he not know?" That must have been one hell of a love spell to ensure that someone as powerful as the High Warlock was not able to see the person he was having sex with or feel their connection.

"Well, they didn't grow up together," my mom explained. "Eloisa herself was the product of an affair, so she didn't spend her childhood here in town. Her mother took her far away and no one really knew who she or who her biological father were. But when Eloisa returned to join our Coven twenty-something years later, she seduced the High Warlock. At the time no one cared, until she was suddenly pregnant—and her blood lines revealed."

Bella shook her head, understanding dawning upon her. "That's *why* he couldn't marry her."

"Exactly," Sherie said. "He probably would have, even though he didn't love her, for the sake of Tabitha. But it was literally impossible given the revelations."

"And she still kept the baby?" I asked, shocked at the stupidity of the woman. "Something could have been *really* wrong with the fetus. Like... genetically."

Mom blew out her breath. "Don't we know it! From what I was told, Eloisa disappeared after her parentage was revealed and returned six months later, babe in arms."

"What did the High Warlock have to say?" Bella asked.

I glanced around the room. The tension was high. Nothing like incest, gossip, and intrigue to keep a group of women engrossed in a conversation.

Sherie shrugged. "What could he say? The child was already born. So, everything was just hushed up. Eloisa was told to keep quiet about her biological father and everyone just went on with their lives. Or so we thought."

I shook my head. "Eloisa must have been obsessed with the High Warlock to do such a sick thing. To seduce her own brother, then cast spells to destroy the wolf pack from the next town."

"All because she was jealous of her brother's love for another woman," Ruby said, filling in the blanks. "Yuck."

The door opened and Fin popped his head in. "Everything okay in here, ladies?"

I nodded, strolling over to my gorgeous mate. "Yeah, we're all good." *Though our moms just revealed a pretty disturbing piece of information.*

Fin grabbed my hand, entwining our fingers and pulling me into his side. "The guys want to go celebrate. And we want you to come meet our parents. Can you do that? Or do you have to stay here...?" He glanced at my mom and the other women behind me.

I turned to them and raised an eyebrow. "I think we deserve the night off to celebrate the win, don't you? We have Ruby back, her baby is safe, and the pack is saved. Surely, we can attack the dad problem tomorrow?"

Truthfully, part of me wanted to work it all out *now*. After all, our fathers deserved just as much focus and sacrifice as we'd dedicated to saving the pack and Ruby today. But given the insanity of what had just come to light, I needed time out. Just a short one.

Ruby brushed back her hair. "Definitely. Don't know about you guys, but I'm exhausted and hungry, and want to crawl into bed with my mates and thank Fate and everyone else," she said, sending a smile my way, "who saved me and my baby today."

My stomach grumbled. "I definitely should have some breakfast soon."

"It's past lunch time now," Fin said, "but Milly's has an all-day breakfast menu. And my mom's house isn't far from there."

I grinned at him. Milly's was in the center of town. No one's place was far from there. "Sounds great."

We all dispersed.

The moms stayed to cook in Ruby's kitchen and chat with our dads about everything that had happened.

Meanwhile, Bella's mates whisked her off, saying something about wanting to see their new house, but I was pretty sure they were just dragging her home to bed.

How Bella got lucky enough to score three mates that constantly wanted to have sex with her, was beyond me. She was the last one I would have thought to have horny Alphas all over her, but maybe that was just my jealousy talking. On the flip side, my mates were dragging me to meet their moms. *That's pretty special, I guess.*

I groaned to myself as I was led out the door to Milly's for a massive late lunch that consisted of way too many pancakes and delicious, frothy milkshakes.

Meeting three mothers-in-law in one afternoon was not something I'd ever expected to have to do in my lifetime, but it wasn't as bad as I thought it would be. The pack as a whole were all in a state of elation, and my future mothers-in-law were just grateful their sons had finally found a mate. The fact that I was a witch didn't seem to worry any of them at all.

By the time dinner rolled around, I was exhausted in a bone-deep way that only a long night's sleep was going to fix. "I think I'm going to head home," I told the guys as we stood outside Milly's once more. "I need my own bed, and preferably one of my mom's amazing home-cooked meals."

When I said home cooked, I meant magicked up, but still. My mom made the best ribs, chicken, and soups, and stews. I wanted something hot and soothing before I succumbed to a deep, desperately needed sleep.

"Can we come with you?" Jase asked casually.

My mouth dropped open. "Really? You want to come to Mom's house with me?"

"Yeah, of course." Fin stepped closer and threw an arm over my shoulders.

"How big is your bed?" Ollie chimed in, the light of excitement flaring in his eyes. "Can we sleep over?" He waggled his eyebrows suggestively.

I got the distinct feeling he wasn't thinking about sleeping. I laughed as heat bloomed in my belly. Despite my exhaustion, I could definitely go for another session with my mates. As long as it didn't last *all* night. Not tonight, anyway. "Let me just check with my mom. I'd love you guys to all be able to come back and sleep at my place." I pulled out my cell phone from my pocket and texted Mom. My bed was only queen sized, but a little magic would fix that up no problem.

Mom replied that she would be home late, if not early in the morning. She had plans with Kathy and Sherie to brew up some potions that might help our dads with their shifting abilities.

I quickly told her I was bringing the guys home to sleep, and that I'd see her in the morning. I waited with bated breath to see her reply,

But it seems I didn't need to worry at all. She just sent through a smiling emoji with hearts for eyes, which made my anxiety swim away. She was fine with me bringing my three soul mates back to our house.

Which means I might get more than a good night's kiss from them all! "It's all good. We can go," I said, grinning as I slid my cell into the back pocket of my jeans.

"Great. I'll drive," Jase said, grabbing onto my hand and pulling me down the street.

I wasn't as good as my mom was with food and recipes, but I could magic up a few pizzas, I was sure. Enough for dinner tonight anyway.

The drive home was relatively quiet, and I shut my eyes for most of the trip. It really had been the most massive day. And Christmas was only a couple of days away. Though, this one wouldn't be quite the same as all the others. I now already had the only thing I had ever wanted. I wondered what Santa might bring me to top this.

"You're going to have to direct me, sweetheart. Sorry," Jase said quietly. "I don't know how to get to your mom's house."

I opened my eyes and shook myself awake. "Yes! Of course. Sorry." I directed Jase to the small house I loved. The one I'd spent my whole life growing up in. Mom had worked her ass to the bone to pay it off, and I admired her so much for her courage in being a single parent. It wasn't something I thought I had the guts to do, and hopefully I never would have to face parenting alone when the time came.

"This is it?" Ollie asked from the back seat. "You sure it's going to fit us all?"

I blew a raspberry at Ollie. "I know it looks tiny, but you'll be fine."

From the outside the house looked a little like a dollhouse, with intricate lacing around the porch and only a single window to the right of the front door. But my mom had extended the back, and my bedroom was huge.

I led the guys inside and we all sat around the small kitchen table. "Pizza?" I asked, lifting my hands up and wriggling my fingers. "And what sort?"

The guys excitedly called out a collection of requests and extra toppings.

In two seconds flat, I magicked up dinner for us all.

"Whoa."

"That's awesome."

They all laughed as large pizzas materialized out of thin air.

I grimaced at the end product. "I'm sorry if they're a bit overcooked. My mom's the chef in the family. Not me. I'm more of a survival cook when it comes to food."

"No. It's perfect," they all chorused and hoed into the food.

Ten minutes later, the pizzas were gone. And I was finally full. I staggered up the stairs to show the guys my bedroom. I pushed open the door, already lifting my hand to magic up the biggest bed I could fit in this room. "Give me one sec, and I'll fix our sleeping arrangements." I wriggled my fingers and sent an expansion spell at my bed.

The mattress widened and the pillows elongated. I pushed it all the way to the edge of both sides of my room, then stopped. It wasn't quite the size of two king beds pushed together, but it would do for tonight. "What do you think?" I asked, waving my arms at the end result like a game show host.

Ollie chuckled and swept me up in his arms.

I squealed as my feet left the ground and grabbed hold of his neck, scared he'd drop me.

He walked over to the bed that still held my woven purple blanket Bella's mom had made for me last Christmas and dumped me down onto the mattress. "You want to go to sleep straight away?" Ollie asked, then reached over his shoulder and tugged his shirt over his head.

That's not fair. My mouth ran dry at the sight of his bare chest. The beauty of him. He had a light sprinkling of hair over thick, perfect muscles. "Well, not straight away," I teased. "Why?"

Ollie chuckled, then pushed his jeans down his thighs. "Because I can't wait to fuck you again." He grinned at me.

All my insides burned with instant heat and I chewed on my lower lip.

Then he stopped, and his smile fell. "Unless you can't...? Then of course I'll wait. I didn't mean—"

Damn, the man was way too hot to be that thoughtful as well. Instead of expressing my thoughts with words, I walked forward, dropped down on my knees, and did something I'd wanted to do since I first saw Ollie naked.

I sucked his cock.

CHAPTER 19

TIFFANY

Taking Ollie's cock in my hand, I leaned forward to wrap my mouth around the head. It was about the bravest thing I'd ever done. My heart pounded like it had the power of a steam engine behind it and my anxiety over being rejected had my stomach tying itself into twisty knots.

A single long groan from Ollie as he slipped his fingers through my hair and gripped me tight to him had my worries melting away. "*Fuck...* Tiff. That. Is. So. Perfect."

I moved up and down his shaft, loving the heat and softness of his skin beneath my tongue—the feel of him in my mouth—and the musky scent of him in my nose.

The other two guys moved around us.

And when I lifted my head to see what they were doing, I found that they were standing next to Ollie, naked too. And waiting their turn. Glancing up, I met Jase's gaze. Lust burned in his eyes. I kissed the end of Ollie's cock and turned toward Jase, ready to taste my second cock.

He stepped closer, thrusting his hips out so I could easily grab hold of his shaft.

I tugged his flesh into my mouth. Jase tasted different to Ollie, somehow. Sweeter, smoother. The difference intrigued and titillated me, and I felt myself growing even wetter between my thighs in response. I sucked and teased, treating him with the same attention I had Ollie.

Then Fin stepped closer, hungry for his turn.

I smiled as I took my final mate's cock into my warm mouth. Fin was the hardest by far. Waiting his turn hadn't done anything to dampen his desire.

I had only managed a few sensuous licks of his long, delicious cock before he interrupted me.

He lifted me up and carried me to bed. "You need to be naked, too," he growled.

I couldn't agree more. I was so ready for this. I started to lift my hips and pull at my jeans, when I realized I had magic at my fingertips. *Jeepers, Tiffany!* I chastised myself. Without a second thought I clicked my fingers and made all my clothes disappear, sending them all to the wash basket in the laundry; a neat trick I'd learned as a teenager. But back then it had been for practicality, not sexuality...

"That's more like it," Ollie said, lying down beside me. He went straight for my breasts, cupping them and setting his lips to my nipples.

I gasped at the strange, new, and pleasurable feeling and grabbed for his head, holding him closer, tighter, wanting more.

He didn't disappoint. Suckling deeply, he forced me to arch my back to get even closer.

Fin lay down on the other side of me and slid his hand between my legs while he kissed me.

I turned my head to give him better access to my mouth, opening for him in every way he wanted. I shivered with need and anticipation. It's finally happening... after the years of hurt and rejection I'd lived with, it was really happening; and it felt wonderful!

His fingers slipped deftly over my clit and between my folds,

I gasped against his mouth as my desire for them grew even higher and more intense. It was literally unlike anything I'd ever experienced.

Fin's fingers masterfully manipulated me like he had it down to an artform. around and around his hand moved, making me climb the peak of my ecstasy higher still.

Ollie's mouth continued to love on my breasts with an ardent passion.

I moaned aloud, unashamed, grabbing for my men, wanting them closer.

"Come here," Ollie said, rolling back and away from me. "Climb on top."

I kissed Fin once more before climbing over to Ollie and instinctively throwing my leg over his waist.

He grabbed my hips and lifted me up and back.

I quickly got the idea and tilted my hips for him, reveling in the feel of him as his cock slid beneath me.

"Damn, I need you," he ground out, a note of feral lust in his voice.

I stared down at him as I tilted back, engulfing his cock slowly, one inch at a time, before sliding down until I was completely stretched beyond belief. I gasped out, throwing my head back. I could scarcely believe it. Ollie was inside me. *I'm not a virgin anymore!*

"Hey beautiful. Want to come all together, tonight?" Jase asked with a gleam in his eye.

I glanced left and right, finding Jase and Fin positioned on either side of me, standing on the bed, their cocks seductively at my eye level.

"How...?" I began to ask.

"Use your hands," Fin said, thrusting his hips forward so that I understood.

I nodded and reached for them, wrapping my fingers around each of their cocks; grateful they were being open and understanding about just how new this all was to me.

Fin and Jase groaned in unison.

Ollie seized me around the waist and thrust up into me.

I moaned with pleasure, feeling the heat of the room begin to over-whelm me. The smell of sex was everywhere. The men above and below me moaned with pleasure as I rode and stroked their cocks with fervor.

"Fuck! I'm going to blow soon. You're *too* fucking hot... my mate," Ollie groaned beneath me,

I felt the tightening of my own orgasm building within my belly and I bore down harder, desperate to take as much of him as I could.

Ollie cried out as he flooded me with his seed.

The warm pulses of his orgasm filled me, and I gasped at the unparalleled pleasure that tore through my body. Glancing down at my mate, a rush of love overwhelmed me at seeing the tortured expression of pleasure on his face.

He squeezed his eyes shut tightly as he fell into his post-orgasm bliss. Then he opened his eyes and they were glazed with lust and emotion.

I grinned at him. "I love making you come." And I meant it. It might be my first time with a man, but it felt special to share some-thing so raw and deep; and not just with any guy, but with someone who just so happened to be one of my three Fates Mates.

He chuckled. "You're far too beautiful for me."

I glanced up at my other two mates, their cocks were thick and swollen with my frantic attempts at mid-coitus stroking. "What should we do now?"

Jase and Fin stared at each other for a minute, then looked down at me. "Do you think you could take us both at the same time?" they said together.

"Um... you mean—" I was pretty sure they meant by putting one of them in my ass, and although that sounded almost *impossible* to imag-ine, I'd quizzed Ruby on the concept, and she'd told me the spell she'd used to make it easy and pain-free.

I chewed on my lip, a thrill of anxiety racing through me as I nodded. "I can do that."

Fin's eyes widened, then he jumped down and off the bed. "Where's the lube?"

I laughed and shook my head. "We don't need it. I can use a spell instead." I carefully eased off Ollie's sated cock.

With a lazy, satisfied smile, the most dominant of my three Betas rolled out of the way.

Jase flopped down onto the bed, on his back. "Jump on, beautiful. Let's see if we can make you cum."

I wanted that too. I ached deep inside my belly with emptiness and need. Ollie had brought me close, but not all the way and I craved that same release. I climbed on top of Jase, my thighs trembling.

He grabbed his own cock, slid me backwards, and pulled me down onto his shaft without pretense.

I gasped at the pressure and pain that came with taking him so quickly.

"I won't last long," he promised, groaning as he grabbed tight to my hips. "Your pussy is fucking divine, Tiffany."

I would have blushed if I could have, but in that moment all my blood seemed to be centered deep in my pussy, throbbing with a heartbeat of its own around Jase's thick cock.

Fin put his hand on my lower back, then slid his fingers down to open my ass cheeks. "You sure about this, sweetheart?" he pressed.

His concern was sweet, but I nodded and said the short spell Ruby had taught me. It would lube me up and take away the pain—or so she said.

"Yes. Please. I want to feel you."

Fin pressed the head of his cock to my asshole and pushed forward.

I gasped, waiting for the pain I was sure would inevitably follow, but instead there was only the delicious slide of his cock inside me, opening me up, and filling me. I closed my eyes at the warring sensations and leaned forward, loving the feel of Jase's kisses on my neck and face.

"Please," I whispered to him. "You need to move." I was as full as I could get, with the perfect pressure on all my pleasure spots, but without them doing more, I was never going to reach climax.

Both men obeyed my request, pulling out, before thrusting back into me with perfect timing.

I cried out at the feeling of being so horribly empty, then so deliciously full a moment later. It was a beautiful, yet agonizing torture.

They began to move faster, picking up pace as they fucked me together.

I moaned, over and over again, until I was a blithering mess of incoherent sounds and gasps. Then my first orgasm crashed over me with an unexpected brutality, and I screamed, shuddering between my two mates.

Jase began to thrust up into me harder and faster, punishing my clit over and over. Seconds later he cried out and thrust up with wild abandon, coming inside me.

His orgasm set off a second round of orgasms within my belly, making my pussy convulse and clench with a chaotic and breath-taking rhythm. I bit my lip as I convulsed in raptures.

Fin groaned, a primitive *growly* sound, as he sunk deep into my ass and came, too.

He was so deep I felt his balls slap against me as they spasmed and shot his seed deep inside me. Scarcely a heartbeat had passed when I felt a hand in my hair and knew it was Ollie, moving closer to be a part of this amazing moment. Collapsing down onto Jase's chest, I opened my eyes.

Ollie gazed down at me, love written all over his face. He bent and dropped a kiss on my swollen lips. "That was incredibly hot," he whispered to me.

I couldn't help but laugh. It *had* been hot. Hotter than I had ever imagined sex could be.

Fin slipped from my body, as starry eyed as Ollie.

Jase carried me to the ensuite shower.

We all washed quickly, then staggered back to my bed and fell into a pile of well satisfied, orgasm and hot shower relaxed bodies.

I was asleep before the covers were pulled up. I'd never been so happy.

~

WHEN I WOKE up the next morning, something had changed—and it wasn't for the better. I reached out for Jase, who was closest to me, and shook his arm. "Hey, we've got to get up. Something's wrong." My stomach twisted when Jase didn't respond. I sat up, looking to my right where Ollie lay stretched out over the bottom half of the bed. "Hey!" I called out to my triad of men. "Are you guys, okay?"

They groaned as a whole, all three of them opening their eyes and slowly pulling themselves up into a seated position.

Oh, thank God for that. They were just sound asleep.

"It's early," Ollie moaned, stretching his arms over his head.

"What's wrong, beautiful?" Jase asked, sliding closer. He pressed a tender kiss to my bare shoulder.

I took a moment to enjoy this incredible feeling, this experience I'd been gifted by Fate, one I'd been dreaming of for *so* long. Of waking up surrounded by heat and flesh and muscles. Three men in my bed who would love me, in time. *Hopefully.*

"I don't know," I said, answering Jase's question. "But something's wrong. I can just feel it. I might go check on my mom. See if she's okay." I didn't know what made me think of my mom, first, but I didn't question my intuition. It was a witch's best friend, according to, well, everyone.

I slid out of the bed and grabbed my robe from the back of the door. My stomach rolled like I was going to be sick, and my skin crawled with a worrying sense of premonition. I glanced back at my bed.

Fin was laying on his belly staring at me with big sad puppy dog eyes.

I had to assume because I'd left without cuddles or kisses.

Jase pushed his long hair out of his eyes, looking sexier than any man had the right to.

Ollie was leaning back on his arms, displaying his gorgeous body to me.

I groaned in frustration but turned away with determination. "I'll be right back!" What sort of sane woman got out of her bed when it contained three men who were naked and probably hoping for good-morning-sex?

I slapped myself in the forehead as I hurried down the stairs. I was crazy to be doing this. But I would just check on my mom, where she would be sleeping safely in her bed on the first floor, then I would run back upstairs to my mates. *I might need to use that lubricating and pain killer spell again,* I mused. I was a little sore in my nether regions if I was being perfectly honest. Three scorching hot wolf shifters was a lot to handle!

I pushed open her door, adjusting my robe as I went. I was still naked beneath, which made this that much more inappropriate. "Mom?" I whispered. If she was sound asleep, I didn't want to wake her. I also didn't want to shock the hell out of her by creeping into her bedroom at what felt like the middle of the night.

Frightening a witch never ended well.

I stepped into her darkened bedroom and glanced at the clock beside her bed. It was seven in the morning. *Not too early. Good.* Then my gaze fell on her bed. It hadn't been slept in. The seventeen hundred pillows she slept with were undisturbed and still piled perfectly in the middle of the mattress.

As I turned to go back upstairs another shiver of premonition shivered through me.

Mom hadn't come home last night. That wasn't the indication that something was wrong. After all, she'd been with her two best friends last night, and my father was in wolf form nearby. They could have fallen asleep on the couches, or they could still be up drinking and chatting. *Who knew with those three?*

But as I ran upstairs to get my cell phone, I had to swallow down the bile that rose. Terrible thoughts surfaced in my mind, unbidden. No matter what happened, I couldn't lose my mom. She'd been my only parent, my rock, my entire life. I hit the green button to call her. The phone went immediately to voice mail... She never turned off her phone.

I hit my mental panic button and started yelling for the guys. "Get dressed. We need to go!" Something was very wrong. It was Christmas Eve, and everything inside my witchy body told me I had to find my mom—and now.

CHAPTER 20

JASE

"It's okay. Sweetheart, just breathe." I concentrated on the road, and not the sound of my mate hyperventilating in the passenger seat next to me. I was already driving as fast as I safely could at twice the speed limit. I couldn't go any faster without killing us all, so I tried to keep Tiffany calm.

Back at the house, she'd run upstairs to tell us that something was wrong with her mom, and that we had to go back to the pack right away. We'd all thrown on our clothes and dashed to the car at her command. She was the queen of our world and if she said move—we did.

When we asked her what was wrong with her mom, she'd started to tremble and couldn't tell us. I wasn't sure if she even knew what was going on. Tiffany was pale and sweating and shaking like a leaf in the breeze. That couldn't be a good sign, surely? But what did I know about witches, anyway? Except that they were powerful and beautiful and loving.

I hoped that when we arrived at Ruby's house, all the moms would just be sitting around with their phones off, chatting away, simply engrossed in conversation and good company and nothing more.

Those women looked like firm friends that could talk an entire day away if they set their minds to it. And in this instance, perhaps it was the whole night?

"Have you heard from anyone else this morning?" Ollie asked tentatively. "Has Ruby or any of the others contacted you?"

Tiff pulled out her cell phone in a flurry from her purse and started typing madly. "You're right. They were at Ruby's house. She should know if something's wrong with my mom!" She smiled at me, though she still trembled, before her concentration returned to tapping away at her phone.

"We're almost there, Tiff," I said, slowing down to pull into the main road that led right up to the town at the heart of pack's territory.

"You're right. I know you're right," she said reassuring herself. "We'll arrive at Ruby's and Mom will be fine. She'll be asleep. Her phone battery probably died overnight. I'm worrying about *nothing*." She combed her hair up into a ponytail with her fingers, then pulled it down again seconds later.

My heart pounded a little bit harder as we stopped outside Ruby's house.

Tiff launched herself out of the car and ran for the front door like an Olympian.

I glanced at the clock on the dashboard. It was barely seven-thirty in the morning. I looked over my shoulder at the guys in the backseat. "I hope they're all awake."

Ollie chuckled. "They will be soon enough if they're not already."

Fin sighed. "Come on. We better get in there."

We all got out of the car and began walking up to the front steps.

I sniffed the air, inhaling deeply, my wolf senses kicking into overdrive. "Tiff's right," I said. "Something's wrong. Can you guys' smell that, too?"

There was a scent on the breeze, like acid.

Ollie sniffed the air, then concern washed over his features. He charged for the front door and swung it open with an almighty slam as he darted inside.

Sharing a fleeting, worried glance, Fin and I followed shortly after.

Inside, nothing seemed out of place, but something seemed off about the house. "Where are they all?" I asked.

The house was clean and eerily quiet.

A bedroom door opened and Jackson walked out completely naked.

Not that I particularly cared. As shifters, we were used to seeing each other naked all the time. It was an entirely natural part of life when you constantly shifted between one form and another.

Tiffany shrieked and covered her eyes.

I realized she felt quite differently about the matter.

"What's going on?" Jackson mumbled sleepily. "Not that it's a problem, but what are you guys doing in my house this early?"

Tiffany turned away with a strange, strangled sound. She said, while facing the kitchen, "I'm sorry we barged in like this, but I have this *really* bad feeling something's wrong with my mom."

Ruby appeared from behind Jackson seconds after, wearing a long black t-shirt that obviously belonged to one of her mates. Thankfully, it was long enough to cover her modesty. It fell all the way to her knees.

"What's going on, Tiff?" she asked, then she turned to her mate with a wry grin. "Go put some clothes on, Jackson. Tiffany doesn't want to see all of that."

Jackson shrugged and headed back into the bedroom as asked.

Ruby walked around Jackson and up to her best friend. "Tiff, what's going on?"

Tiffany turned around, her eyes brimming with unshed tears. "Something's wrong with my mom. I just know it. I'm probably being silly. Please tell me I'm being silly. Where are they?" she begged, the words practically tumbling out of her.

Ruby frowned and ran a hand through her tangled long red hair. "What do you mean, where are they?"

Uh-oh.

"I thought they were with you guys," Ruby said. "As in, I thought Rebecca had gone home. We went to bed around midnight and the three moms were still at it, talking and mixing spells. Didn't she come home sometime during the early hours?"

Tiffany shook her head, tears falling down her cheeks now. "No, she didn't. Her bed hasn't been slept in and I woke up with the worst feeling of dread."

Ruby tilted her head to the side. "You know the moms sometimes have sleepovers. Could your mom have maybe gone back to Kathy's place since you texted to say that you were going home with your guys? Perhaps she just didn't want to... intrude, you know?"

Tiffany brightened instantly, a smile stretching across her lips. "Oh my God. You're probably right! Of course, Mom wouldn't want to come back to our house if she knew I was there with my mates." She smacked her forehead as she flushed a rosy shade of pink. "I'll message Kathy right now and see what they're doing."

I sniffed the air again. Something still wasn't right, though. "Ruby, do you mind if I check out the back?"

Ruby's eyebrows flicked up, but she didn't deny my request. "Yeah, of course I don't mind. Do you want to go see the dads?"

I nodded, because what else was I going to say? That I, too, had a feeling of premonition that something was seriously wrong? "Thanks." I went in the direction she pointed, through the kitchen and the laundry. The back door put me straight onto the porch.

I stopped and stared at the carnage before me.

All three moms were laying on the grass beside each of their wolves, in various positions of defensiveness. There was some smoke and fire damage to the grass, and from what I could tell there had been one hell of a fight.

I ran a hand through my hair. "Fucking hell!"

Tiffany's mom was lying on her side with her wolf mate half covering her protectively. He had blood caked into his fur all the way along his ribs.

I turned back to the house and called out. "Tiff! Ruby! You guys need to come out here. *Now.*"

The back door swung open. Tiffany walked out, her brow furrowed in confusion.

I reached for her just as she saw what lay on the back grass.

She let loose a sob that broke my heart as her knees gave way and she crumpled.

I grabbed for her and held her against me, stopping her from falling to the ground.

Ruby came up behind us. "What's going on? Holy shit!" She ran down the stairs and fell to her knees beside her parents reaching for her mom to check for a pulse.

I held Tiffany's sobbing form to me tightly and called out to the guys inside. "Ollie! Get Jackson and the other guys. Quick." I turned back to Ruby, who seemed a lot calmer than Tiffany.

She crawled from one witch to another, gently petting each wolf as she went.

"Are they alive?" I asked, terrified on Tiff's behalf, for the answer. How was Tiffany going to survive losing her mom *and* her dad, especially before she'd even gotten a chance to know him?

Ruby nodded, pressing the back of her hand to her nose, I assumed to stop herself from crying. "They're alive. Just."

Jackson and Billy burst through the door. They scooped up Ruby and carried her back to the porch and away from the macabre display before us.

We all stood together, staring at the bodies laid out on the lawn.

"Should we get some help?" I asked. "Or blankets? An ambulance? What do we do here?"

Wolf shifters were rarely sick as a rule, until they died. We didn't have many doctors, nor did we use the local hospital for anything other than the women birthing babies. Or if someone had experienced a minor injuring or cut off a finger.

Tiffany wiped at her face and gulped. "This is the work of a warlock. Or a witch. We can't do anything, except kill the one responsible."

I lifted her face to mine by raising up her chin. "What do you mean? *Who* did this?"

She bit her trembling lip and shook her head. "We don't know. I don't know... I don't know..."

I pulled her in close, hoping the warmth of my body would comfort her in some small way. "What should we do, Ruby?" I asked.

She shuddered in Jackson's arms.

Fin and Ollie rushed outside, reaching for Tiffany.

I handed her over to them. "Go on. Take her inside. She's freezing." I turned back to Ruby.

She looked pale and exhausted.

"What can we do?"

Her keen gaze rose and met mine. "It looks like there was a fight of some sort and an explosion. Someone set off a spell. Maybe it was intended to kill them, I can't be sure. Either way, they didn't succeed, and have instead put them all into an unconscious state." She shook her head as though trying to clear her thoughts. "We need to get Bella." Her eyes were unfocused now. "She'll know what to do. She's the brains." Ruby turned to go inside.

Bella would probably be at her place with her three mates. Hopefully, she was well enough to diagnose the problem and work out the solution. She'd already almost died looking for answers.

I flicked my gaze back to the yard and the occupants still lying on the grass as though they were asleep. *What the hell have we gotten ourselves into?*

TIFFANY

I shook all over, with fear more than anything else. Who had done this to our parents?

Fin and Ollie held me in their laps on the couch, trying to warm me,

But I still couldn't stop shivering—and it wasn't just the cold.

Ruby walked into the kitchen and grabbed her cell phone.

I pushed out of Ollie's arms and staggered to my feet. "Who are you calling?"

Ruby put the phone to her ear. "Bella. Surely, she can work out what's happened... Hey Bella. Sorry to wake you. Yeah, can you feel it?"

I stared at her. Did the other two feel the same creeping premonition that I had this morning?

"Ah-huh. You need to get over here ASAP, Bell. No, I won't tell you on the phone, just get your butt over here and—"

Before Ruby could finish the sentence, Bella materialized in the lounge room.

She put her hands on her hips. "What are you doing here so early, Tiff? Shouldn't you be celebrating with your new mates somewhere?"

I swallowed hard so I didn't cry. "I woke up and I knew something was wrong. I checked Mom's bedroom and she hadn't slept in it all night. So, I called her, and you know my mom always has her phone on because she's on call for work all the time."

Bella dropped her arms at her side. "Well, where is she then?"

I sniffed to stop the tears from leaking out of my eyes. "She's in the back yard. They all are."

"What do you mean, they all are?" Bella's eyes grew wide, then she bolted for the back door like a bird on the wing.

We all followed but didn't get to her in time to warn her.

Her yell of anguish sounded through the air as she threw herself toward her mom and dad.

I pushed open the back door.

Bella ran her hands all over her mom, from her ankles to her waist, to her neck, then her hands.

What she was looking for, I didn't know. I'd skipped so many parts of magic class when I was at school, I was lucky I knew what I did. "What's she doing?" I finally asked Ruby, then turned as the back door opened again.

"Coffee?" Darren asked, holding a mug out to each of us.

Ruby took hers with a grateful smile.

I grabbed for mine. "Thank you so much." Boy, did I need it this morning. I added some sugar with a wiggle of my magical fingers, then turned back to the surreal and bloody scene that had rocked us to our cores.

Bella was crawling from one mother to another, checking each of them for signs of... something.

"I think she's trying to diagnose what's wrong with them," Ruby suggested, then took a sip of her coffee.

Steam rose off the top of my mug, and I blew on it once, before wrapping one arm around my middle. I still felt sick to my stomach and couldn't shake it.

"What do you think it is?" I asked. "Poison? Or just the aftershocks of a powerful blast?"

Ruby shook her head. "Truthfully? No idea, though it looks like someone waged one hell of a battle out here."

The more I looked, the more evidence I saw that proved Ruby's suspicions. There were black scorch marks on the grass and even on some of the fur on the wolves. Mine and Bella's fathers had blood in their fur, and yet everyone still appeared to be breathing—*at least for now.*

"What do you think it was, Bell?" Ruby called out. "Do you want a coffee or anything?"

Bella got to her feet, dusted the grass off her hands and the tears off her cheeks. "No. I'm okay." She walked over to the porch and shivered from the cold. "Let's go inside."

We followed her in, where all the mates were sitting, including Bella's three.

Jackson and Darren were in the kitchen, frying up bacon from the smell of the room.

Meanwhile, the three of us girls huddled on a single couch, holding hands like we used to when we were little.

I trembled with an invasive shot of fear that passed through me. These girls were all I had left if my mom died.

"Stop thinking the worst," Bella said, squeezing my hand.

I smiled at her meekly. "Stop reading my mind."

"What do you think it is, Bella?" Ruby asked again. "What can we do?"

Bella sighed. "I think they were in an epic battle last night. How you didn't hear anything, Ruby? I have no freaking idea."

Ruby nodded, guilt written all over her face. "I don't know how we didn't hear anything, either. When we went to bed and all three of our moms were just chatting, cooking, and making a potion. Bella's mom was reading a spell book..." Ruby stopped, then jumped to her feet.

"What is it, Ruby?" I asked.

"The book! It was full of location spells. I bet they tried to find Tabitha, or Eloisa, or both." She ran for the kitchen and started pulling out drawers, then rushed to the corner pantry. "Where would they have put it?" she fussed. "Oh. Here! Got it!" She pulled a massive tome of a book off one of the high shelves, then staggered with it.

Jackson grabbed it from her and helped her carry it over to the coffee table. He dropped it down on the table and it made a loud thumping noise.

I jumped, even though I'd been expecting it. I was really jangled.

"That is one hell of a heavy book!" Jackson remarked.

"Thanks, hon," Ruby said to her massive mountain of a man.

He grinned in return and headed back to the kitchen to keep feeding the troops.

I gazed over to my own mates anxiously.

In between bites of hot food and sips of steaming coffee, kept shooting me looks of mutual concern.

Ruby kneeled on the carpet and flicked through the pages of the book. "Here it is." She tapped on a spell in front of her. "Just before I went to bed, I saw this over my mom's shoulder. It was this symbol that caught my eye." She pointed at the picture at the top of the page. "This is what they must have been doing last night."

Bella lowered herself to her knees and pulled the book toward her, reading the page rapidly. She gasped, her hand flying to her mouth in shock. "They *wouldn't.*"

"What is it?" I pressed as my stomach twisted itself in knots.

"It's a location spell, but one that is only intended for those that you can't find any other way. It literally tears that person out of their life and whatever they're doing and sets them right in front of you. If Tabitha had that happen to her, I would have to say she'd be the kind of witch to shoot first and ask questions later."

"You think she tried to kill our parents?" I asked, aghast. *What a psychotic monster!*

Bella nodded and shook her head in dismay. "It's not a stretch to imagine, Tiff."

Ruby frowned. "But then why are they all still alive?"

Bella ran a hand through her hair. "Because our moms are

powerful witches who would have put up preemptive barriers. That would account for why you couldn't hear them, Ruby. I bet they put up a protective bubble, or something, and they were essentially sound-proofed."

Ruby leaned back against the couch. "Oh, thank God for that. I thought there was something seriously wrong with me; that I could have done something to…"

Bella shook her head and reached out a hand to our best friend. "It's not your fault, Ruby. But this does beg one question."

"What's that?" I asked, trying desperately to find my courage for the sake of our mothers.

"How fucking powerful is this witch?" she finished.

I burst out laughing. I couldn't help it. Bella never swore, not like that anyway.

"What?" Bella said, her lips twitching at the sides. Though she knew exactly what I found funny.

"Nothing. Sorry. You're right. How fucking powerful is she? And is the 'she' Tabitha? Are you sure it isn't *her* mom?"

Ruby pushed herself up so she could sit back on the couch. "Do you really think Tabitha's mom is capable of what happened outside? Isn't she ancient by now?"

I shrugged. "I have no idea. How old would she be anyway? Seventy? But we know one thing—she's capable of some pretty fucked up things. You know what she did with the High Warlock and every-thing. And if she's the product of an affair as well, then no one really knows her parentage either. She could have all sorts of weird stuff in her genes."

Bella and Ruby looked between each other, then nodded.

"You're right," Ruby said. "It could be either of them, so we need to be really careful about how we approach this."

"I don't care about Tabitha *or* Eloisa," I said stiffly. "They can go jump off a cliff for all I care. I just want my mom back and I want my dad too."

"Eloisa and Tabitha are the key to the curse that's holding our dads in wolf form," Bella said. "Unfortunately, I think we're going to have to find them and work out a way to break the link."

I raised an eyebrow. "Break the link? You *know* we don't have any idea how to break that link except through death."

"So, we kill them," Ruby said with a fierce grin. "I'm sure we can manage to do the spell to them that the moms did to us. Their hearts only have to stop for sixty seconds or maybe a little bit longer to break the spell."

I took a minute to think about it. Then I turned to my friends. "Do you think we need to ask the Coven for some help? How are we even going to find them?"

Bella shook her head. "I don't think we should involve anybody else. I believe we can do it ourselves. It's too dangerous to risk involving others. Anyway, this is our battle."

I wasn't so sure we could do it on our own. Our moms were more powerful than us, and yet they were all outside, in comas having been hit with a single spell. Or so we assumed. "Should we ask our mates to help us then?"

"What do you mean?" Ruby asked. "How can they help?"

"I'm just thinking out loud here, but Tabitha and her mom hate the wolves, so that has to give us some sort of advantage, surely? And our moms have used spells before that have had our mates ground us and amplify our magic. Maybe we could try the same spell but be better equipped than our moms went into it?"

I let my idea ruminate for a moment before continuing. "Or we could just leave Tabitha and her mom alone," I suggested, though I was pretty sure this was one of those times where hoping the issue would resolve itself, wouldn't work.

Bella shook her head. "We can't. We need to get them here and break the spells they cast on our moms and dads. Without them, we'll never get our dads back, and we may never be able to wake our moms up again, either," she said matter-of-factly with a chilling edge.

I groaned. *I knew it.* This was all going to come down to a single fight. Them versus us.

"So what are you thinking of for a spell, in regard to us and our mates?" Bella asked me, ever the pragmatic one.

"I didn't have any other ideas on how to actually achieve the practical side of what I was suggesting." I laughed humorlessly. "I was hoping you would know a spell that could do that. You *are* the resident bookworm, after all."

Bella tapped her fingers against her lips in thought. Then she held out her hands in front of her over the coffee table and transported several books from somewhere.

I had to assume they came from her mom's house or her new home with her mates.

"What have you got there?" Ruby asked curiously.

"Books, obviously," Bella said with a grin. "I'm pretty sure I know which spell your mom used, Ruby, to save you on Halloween. She pulled magic from the earth and channeled it through your mates. Because they're shifters and therefore super-strong paranormals, they survived the process. She was able to harness ancient magic through them and pull you back into the realm of the living. Tiffany is right in that we can probably use our mates to bolster our magic and our power so that we don't get wiped off the face of the planet if we try to locate and transport Tabitha to us."

"You seriously think we should do it?" Ruby asked, her mouth open as though she was surprised that we might actually follow through.

Bella opened the books in front of her and flicked through the pages. "Yes, I do. I don't think we have any other choice. We need to wake them up and we need to break this curse once and for all. It all comes down to one single witch and I *know* in my gut that it's Tabitha. It has to be. Eloisa used to be a key player but she's not anymore. She didn't ground any of the spells in herself because she knew she'd die first. It's all based around Tabitha. It just makes the most sense."

"So, Eloisa isn't in the picture?" I asked.

Bella laughed. "We should never discount her mother. You know that moms can be over-protective, especially when they only have a single daughter and no husband to rely on."

I couldn't help but laugh at that one. "That's funny. I've never thought about how much Tabitha and us are alike. You know, except for the fact that she is the product of incest and totally fucked in the head. But I get the fact that she was raised by a single mom who considered her the center of the universe."

I glanced toward the door that led outside into Ruby's backyard where our moms still lay helpless. "Do you think they're okay?" I asked, sobering, then bit my lip at the idea of my mom being in pain. "Or are they, like, torturing them inside their own minds and bodies? Trapped?"

Bella shook her head in denial. "I hope they're in some sort of dream-like sleep."

I hoped so too. I couldn't stand the idea of my mom being trapped and going insane or being in some kind of excruciating pain. "Okay then, so what's the plan?" I asked. "Do the same spell as our moms did last night? We find Tabitha, make her heart stop for one minute—break the spell—and free our parents forever?"

Ruby and Bella glanced at each other, then at me.

Our favorite red-head grinned. "Yeah. Easy, right?"

I rolled my eyes. "Yeah, totally easy." *For a full coven with advanced powers, maybe.*

"We have our mates to ground us and to draw power from, if they'll allow us to," Bella said, tapping a page. "I have the spell right here."

"Okay, so, supercharge our powers using our wolf mates, then do everything I just said," I repeated, my heart pounding in a mixture of fear and excitement.

"And we've got to try not to die," Ruby said, without smiling. "I have a baby onboard, remember."

I groaned. *Shit.* We were dealing with a real lunatic witch after all. That was a possibility. *We might not survive this...* I realized bleakly.

"Okay." I sighed. "So, supercharge, do the spells, and don't die—in that order."

"Yeah, that's pretty much it," Bella said with a grimace.

I covered my face with my hands. *Damn it.* We were never getting out of this in one piece! Just when I'd almost attained everything I'd ever wanted. And it was Christmas, tomorrow, too. *What fucking bad timing is this?*

CHAPTER 22
OLLIE

"You want us to do... *what?*" I blinked at my mate, not sure I understood what she was asking exactly.

We were all sitting around in a 'witch mate' circle. All nine of us crammed into Jackson's lounge room, our three beautiful, unique, and powerful witch mates in the middle of the circle, standing as they explained some crazy plan about taking down a wicked witch.

Tiffany glanced at Ruby.

Ruby sighed. "It's basically..."

Jackson groaned from where he lounged back on the couch. "It's basically crap," he said with an echoing sigh, as he shifted his legs. He was restless and didn't seem able to find a comfortable spot to settle. "It hurts like a bitch, I'll be honest. But if Ruby needs my strength to survive whatever they've got to do to save their parents, then she can have all of it."

I had no idea what to say. It was obvious that Jackson and some of the other guys had been through this before. I didn't want to look like a wimp or an idiot but having a witch drain my power or strength kind of scared the shit out of me. I glanced at the other guys who were looking just as worried as I was. At least I wasn't alone in my misgivings, which made me feel a little better. This was some seriously heavy shit.

Tiffany sat down on the couch next to me. Then she reached over and took my hand. "Witches get more powerful with time and age," she explained. "Genetics helps too. Ruby and I are only half witches, and we aren't very old. Bella is more powerful than us, but even so, if our three moms ended up like that outside, going up against this one witch? Then there's no way the three of us can take her on and win, without you."

I clenched my jaw and told myself to harden the fuck up. We'd said that we would do whatever Tiffany needed of us. This was what came with being in a mated couple or, in our case, a full family: sacrifice. It was time to put our money where our mouths were. "And it's going to hurt like a bastard, like you said, Jack?"

Jackson laughed, though there wasn't much humor in the sound. "Oh, yeah. Billy and Darren passed out from it last time."

Billy growled at him.

"I think it was only my strength as an Alpha that kept me going, to be fair," Jackson added to calm his Beta.

I had to laugh. "Seriously?"

Billy glared at me. "You won't understand until it's actually done to you."

I tried not to grimace, but I knew that I probably hadn't succeeded when Tiffany stared at my face for too long.

She withdrew her hand and stood up. "It's okay if you can't. It will leave me more vulnerable of course, but if Ruby and Bella have the strength to do the spell, we can probably get through it without your help." Her tone was one of disappointment and understanding all at once and it cracked something inside me.

I grabbed for her hand and pulled her back so that she was sitting on my lap. There was no way I was losing my mate over this. *Not a chance in hell!* We'd gotten into a lot of trouble and had countless injuries throughout our lives already, and ultimately, I wasn't afraid of a little bit of pain. It would be a small price to pay for the love of my mate.

It was just the unknown that terrified me. And the magical element. I knew next to nothing about witches. All of this was new territory. A whole new world.

Fin and Jase reached over and took Tiff's hands in theirs. "We'll do it," they said.

I nodded and tried to ignore the quiver of panic that rose at the idea of what they were talking about. Weren't they anxious too? Or were they simply braver than me? I sighed at the thought. I needed to hold my own. "All right. What else do we need to know?" I asked, turning to the other two witches in the room.

Bella opened the book she'd been holding and pointed to a page with elaborate and intricate pictures and lots of strange, cursive writing.

I couldn't even read it. I assumed it was in some sort of ancient magical language that they could decipher, and we couldn't.

"This spell will help bolster our power through you guys." She flipped a couple of pages, put that book down, then picked up another one. "And this is the spell our moms used the other day to stop our hearts and break the curse on the pack."

"And you intend to do both of those?" I asked, following as closely as I could.

Tiffany nodded. "On different people obviously. We'll have to do 'boosting power' on each other, and then the 'heart stopping' spell will be cast on Tabitha when she arrives."

"What do you mean, *when she arrives*?" Jase asked, one brow furrowed.

Bella gasped. "Oh yeah. Of course, sorry! There's a third spell we need to do as well." She rummaged through the pile of books and finally pulled up a massive Bible-looking thing, with heavy leather binding and old gold lettering. "There's a spell to locate Tabitha—the witch we're looking for. This spell will locate her and physically bring her to us."

Elliot stood. "Is that what your mothers did last night?"

I stared at him. Either he had really in tune instincts or he knew these witches better than I did. I would never have put those two things together.

Bella nodded, her eyes big and round as she stared at Elliot with a measure of pride. "Yes, hon. I think that's what they did, but we weren't here so I'm only guessing."

Elliot grumbled, a deep growl rolling through the room. "So, it's dangerous, Bella?"

She hesitated. "Technically, it is, as you can see from what happened outside. If it's true that this spell is what our moms did, then Tabitha is far more powerful than our moms ever realized."

"Or she just got the drop on them," Tommy offered. "We came up against her at the church over Thanksgiving, and she didn't win that fight. She ran away like a coward."

I didn't know what they were talking about, and I wasn't sure I wanted to know. These witches had been through hell and back over the last few months it seemed. Between finding their mates and trying to save their fathers, not to mention helping our whole pack by breaking the curse, it had been an eventful year to say the least.

"Do you think they can do it?" I asked Elliot, holding his gaze with some trouble. I forced myself to straighten and swallow down any foolish Beta-bowing tendencies my genetics still craved.

Elliot nodded. "Yeah. These girls are made of courage and fire. It's just... Bella's *my* mate..."

Once again, I was struck by how much power these girls had over their mates. We would literally walk over glass for them if we needed to, and it was obvious the other mates already had done so, proving their mettle. They were our greatest gifts and also our undoing. They were our strength and our weaknesses. And losing them would mean our deaths.

My chest ached with the thought. What would I do if Tiffany was hurt or killed? Just get back on the road and try to find another mate? I swallowed the hot, sour bile that rose in my throat. *No fucking way.* She was my one and *only* mate. There would be no other. Ever. I would never love anyone else, and because of that, I would offer up whatever strength my Beta blood gave me. "I can't lose you," I whispered to Tiffany, pressing my nose into her hair and inhaling her cherry sweet scent.

She pulled back and stared at me. "You won't. But we have to do this."

Some of the other guys surged to their feet.

"Well, let's do this then," Tommy said.

Tiffany slipped off my lap and stood with the others.

I glanced at Jase and Fin.

They nodded and clenched their jaws.

"What's the plan?" Tiffany asked Bella.

"We need to find a safe space to channel the energy of our mates, and make sure Tabitha doesn't hurt anyone else."

"I bet that's what our moms did wrong," Ruby said. "They probably put up the protection bubble so they wouldn't affect the pack or wake us up."

Tiffany nodded. "Total waste of a spell and power considering they got blasted after that, anyway."

Bella inhaled sharply, running both hands through her dark hair. "Where to go... where to go? Ah-ha! The church. It has to be. It's the only place I know that's big enough, safe enough, and..."

"The sacred grounds amplify your magic naturally," Darren finished for her.

Everyone turned to look at him.

He flushed a hot red and shrugged. "What? I learned a thing or two the night Ruby almost died on us."

I shuddered and shared a look with Jase. It sounded like all the guys had almost lost their Fated Mate at one time or another. There was obviously a happy ending, because they all stood here happy and well. But I wasn't sure I wanted to go through the same trial by fire all the other mates had needed to. I felt conflicted. Anxious, brave, ready, and afraid all at once and it was maddening! I wasn't used to acknowledging my feelings like the others...

I reached for Tiffany, grabbing her hand for attention. I needed to do *something*. I was feeling impatient and impotent. My wolf clawed at my mind to get out. "What can we do?"

Tiffany bit her lip. "It's probably best if you guys get to the church grounds manually. It'll drain you to be transported."

I nodded. I didn't want to say it out loud, but I definitely didn't want to go through that shit way of traveling again.

"You're right, Tiff," Ruby said. "We need to go together, and transportation would be the quickest. Grab the books and whatever else we need. The guys can shift and run if they want. Or drive, if they want to be boring." She winked at them.

"So, we should go, like, now?" I asked, already beginning to tug at my clothes. My skin was itching for the shift.

Tiffany nodded. "Go. We'll meet you there."

Elliot and Tommy sauntered up, all huge and bold. "We'll go with you."

Darren stepped closer. "I don't need to shift. I'll go with the girls."

I nodded and began to let go of my humanity.

"I'm going to call Maddi and Paula, my mom's friends from the Coven and see if they'll watch over our moms," Ruby said, grabbing for her cell phone and dialing.

I let the shift fully take me. I fell to the floor, my arms turning to legs as gray fur sprouted through my skin.

A huge black wolf appeared in front of me, then a white one.

Whoa. They were fucking big.

They tilted their heads at me.

I followed them out the front door of Ruby's house and into the fresh air, taking a deep breath as Jase and Fin joined me.

Together, we stood shoulder to shoulder.

A part of me still couldn't believe that I was sharing a mate with my two best friends, but at the same time, it was as natural as breathing. We were a family. A team. Our own pack. And today, we were going to help our girl kick ass, and hopefully get her home—still in one piece.

CHAPTER 23

TIFFANY

My two best friends, and Darren, collected everything we needed for the spells: protection charms to wear, crystals for boosting our power, and of course the books that Bella needed to recite the incantations from.

All eight of the other mates shifted into their wolf forms and took off toward the church.

We were left in a lounge room that looked like a fire alarm had gone off. There were shirts, and hoodies, and tanks, and jeans strewn everywhere.

Ruby huffed with a hand on her hip. "Just look at this place."

"Do we need to take any of this with us?" I asked.

Ruby began to giggle.

"What's funny?" I asked.

"Sorry, I was just picturing it. The three of us trying to conduct this super-powerful spell, with a ring of huge, naked men all around us." She stopped to laugh again. "It'll look like some sort of weird, pagan ritual."

I shuddered. I'd only had sex twice now. I wasn't sure I'd be able to focus on the magic I needed to perform if *all* of our well-built mates were standing around us, butt naked. Just seeing Jackson nude for a second this morning had made me feel more embarrassed than I'd ever been in my life. He was Ruby's, not mine. I didn't want to look at all that... stuff. I had my very own to worry about—and was very satisfied. "Okay, so, we'll grab their jeans," I said.

Bella reached for my arm before I went to scoop them all up. "Allow me." She flicked her fingers in the air and all eight pairs of jeans floated up, then she neatly folded them on the couch in a pile.

"Are we almost ready to go, then?" I asked, glancing around at the things we had to take with us. "We look like we might need a car."

Ruby nodded. "Probably a good idea, though we need to wait for Paula to arrive." The doorbell peeled and Ruby grinned. "Never mind, I think she's here. Hopefully, she can cast some sort of stabilizing spell for our moms or think of something to do to help them that we didn't." Ruby set off to open the front door.

I turned to Bella. "Are you okay?"

She nodded. "Of course. Why?"

I grabbed her hand and squeezed it. As she was the most intro-verted and quiet of the three of us, it was easy to assume Bella was fine, when in actuality she probably wasn't. It was always best to check in with her, just in case. "A lot of the stress of this plan has come to rest on your shoulders. I know it's not fair, and I'm sorry I can't do more, Bella."

She turned to me so she could look me in the eye. "I'm fine, honestly. I have you and Ruby, and all our mates there. We're going to do this. We're going to get our lives back to how they should have *always* been. We were robbed in the past. I'll be damned if I lose anything more in the future."

I sniffed as the heat of tears as they tingled in the back of my nose and eyes. "You're right," I said, and hugged her tight. "I believe in you —in us. We can do this."

Ruby walked back into the room.

Behind her followed a pale-looking Paula, a woman I'd seen from past Coven meetings on occasion. She had curly red hair and a dress sense similar to Kathy's. She wore an orange quilted skirt and a bright green flowing blouse. And I intuitively knew we could trust her.

"Paula. You know my friends, Bella and Tiffany," said Ruby.

The older woman ran a frazzled hand through her curly hair. "I do, but I don't think I've spoken to you girls before. It's nice to officially meet you."

"Nice to meet you too," I automatically replied. "Thank you for coming to stay with them. We didn't want to leave our mothers alone."

Paula's eyebrows lowered in a frown. "I can't believe they took on Tabitha and she did this." Paula wrapped her arms around her chest. "I'll do what I can, though I doubt I'll be able to do much more than sit with them."

"That's all we need, today." Bella said quietly. "Thank you for coming on such short notice, Paula."

"We really need to get going, so let me show you where they are. They're just right out here," Ruby said, directing Paula through the lounge room.

I didn't follow. I didn't want to go outside and see my mom like that again. The next time I saw her, I wanted her to be awake, and I wanted to see my dad in human form for the first time. I wanted us to be a family. That was the dream anyway.

"Should we pack the car while we wait for Ruby?" Darren asked, grabbing some water bottles from the fridge. "Or do you guys want to transport there?"

I didn't know which I preferred, but I had a thought on the idea. "Do you think it would maybe be better to save our energy and magic for the big show down?"

Bella picked up one of the books and held it to her chest. "Yeah, I do. Transportation takes quite a bit of magic, and we're going to need every drop we have in reserve."

I nodded at Bella before turning to the half-warlock. "Let's go pack the car then," I said, picking up the pile of eight pairs of jeans. "Who's got the biggest truck?"

Darren chuckled. "Jackson, I think. His keys are in the bedroom. Let me go grab them and we can pack."

After we finished packing up the vehicle, we jumped into Jackson's truck and headed for the church grounds. It took fifteen minutes by car, but the wolves could run straight through the forest, so they'd probably already beaten us there.

"The boys are going to have to wait for us," I said.

"Doesn't matter," Ruby mused, staring out the window. "They can't do anything before we get there, anyway."

I turned to Ruby, a thought occurring to me. "How are you going to do this, Ruby? I mean, how's your magic at the moment?"

Since Halloween a few months ago, Ruby had said her magic was literally gone. She couldn't use it.

I hadn't been sure if that was entirely true, or if her pregnancy simply made her too fearful to even try.

Ruby sighed and wriggled her fingers. "There's magic there. It's been coming back a little every day. But I've been too afraid to try anything. The pregnancy takes *so* much out of me, and I don't know how this is going to go. But I'll give it everything I've got."

Even if that means losing the baby? I wondered to myself.

"We'll be there for you," Darren said from the driver's seat. "All the way. No matter what. You can take all my power, plus more."

Ruby smiled, though I could see the pain and weight of the world in her eyes. "Thanks, honey."

We were quiet for the rest of the drive. When we arrived, a pack of eight wolves prowled around the church car park.

"The zoo's in town," Darren joked, as he drove slowly through the pack.

The wolves dispersed and I watched them in awe. Black, white, and gray. We had all three beautiful colors between us.

As we climbed out of the car, they began to shift back to human form.

I grabbed the pile of jeans from the trunk and threw them toward the men. "We brought your pants!" I looked quickly away. There were so many dicks I just couldn't cope until they were all covered.

"Let's go set up," Ruby said, calling to me from the truck.

I ran to her and grabbed some of the books and crystals, glad to be away from the dick-fest. "Where do you want to put all this?"

"Under the tree where they took me," Ruby said, shivering.

"Where's that?"

"This way." Ruby trudged off behind the church, her arms full of crystals and a blanket.

Bella grabbed the rest of the spell books.

Meanwhile, Darren grabbed everything we hadn't,

Then we all walked over the frost covered grass to stand near the graveyard, where a large tree stood in the middle of nowhere.

"Here?" I asked.

Darren shuddered and put everything down. "Damn, this place has some bad memories attached to it."

Ruby stood, staring at the tree, her hand protectively resting on her stomach.

"Bella," I called out.

She was placing the spell books down and arranging them for the best vantage point.

"Yeah?"

I sighed heavily. *How am I going to say this without offending anyone?* "Do you think we should, I don't know, protect Ruby somehow?"

"What do you mean?" Bella asked, glancing up.

"I'll be fine!" Ruby said with a frown.

I ignored her and focused on Bella. "Ruby hasn't used any magic since Halloween. What if something happens—to her, or the baby? I know you and I can't do it ourselves, but... I'm worried."

Ruby groaned and rolled her eyes. "Ugh. Tiff! Seriously?"

Bella put a hand to her mouth. "Oh, my God. I'd completely forgotten that your magic had taken a leave of absence since you became pregnant."

Ruby threw her hands up in the air in frustration. "I *have* magic! I'm still a bloody witch. I've just been... worried about using it."

I stared at Bella. "So, what do we do?"

Bella bit her lip. "With the magic in the hallowed ground here, and her mates to bolster her, Ruby should be okay to channel all of that into herself. She wouldn't even need to use a lot of her own magic."

Ruby groaned again. "Guys! I can do it."

I turned to her and glared. "Ruby, we didn't save you and your daughter to lose you now. I know you want to do everything you can to save our parents, but we don't want you accidently sacrificing anything in the process. Got it?" I said with conviction. If there was one thing I was good at, it was being independent and standing on my ground when life required it.

Darren stepped closer. "I can help," he said. I've been working on my warlock abilities, and if you can work out a way to channel what magic I have into Ruby, I'll gladly give it up to protect her."

Ruby turned to her warlock-wolf and threw herself into his arms.

I looked at Bella. This was going to come down to *us*. Bella had more raw power, that much was true, but I had the will, and it was made of tempered steel. I wanted my parents back, whole and alive, and human. I didn't care what I had to do, and I could be as stubborn as a mule, if my mom was anyone to go by.

The guys headed toward us, walking around the church like a photoshoot for some sexy magazine. All I could see were huge pecs, tight abs, and great arms strolling in slow motion.

Bella began to arrange everyone into formation—a triangle—the strongest shape; a literal pyramid of power. She grabbed me and moved me over a few feet, then called out to my guys. "Can you three stand behind her, please? One hand on her shoulder."

They all reached out and touched me as instructed.

I shivered at the feeling of their strength against me. I closed my eyes, and a wash of premonition crashed over me. *She's coming,* I realized. She was searching for us. My eyes popped open again. "We need to hurry," I urged Bella. "She's coming. I can feel her."

Bella stared at me for a moment, shock written all over her expression, then picked up her pace. "Ruby, here. Quick. And you guys, hands on her shoulders. My guys, come here. Okay!" She snatched up one of the books when we were all finally in order. "Hold onto your lunches, boys. This is going to get *rough*."

"Do we have to hold on to our mate the whole time?" Ollie called out.

I was glad he asked, because I wanted to know that, too. Would breaking the physical connection jeopardize the success of the plan?

"You don't have to if the pain gets too much," Bella said. "Your nearby presence is enough; but it would help, so hold on as long as you can! Even if you're on the ground and it's just to her ankle. Okay, I'm going to do the translocation spell." Then she pointed to the book in front of me. "I want you to hit her with the heart stopping spell as soon as you've got eyes on her, okay?"

I nodded, fueling my resolve. "I will." I would cast that spell not matter what. I had the earth of my ancestors beneath my feet and the touch and support of my mates around me. My whole fairy tale future with my parents was on the line. I could manage the spell.

"What about me?" Ruby asked.

Bella broke away from her mates to place a book in front of Ruby. "The land here will boost our natural powers anyway, but if you can do this spell, it's the one that will drag our mates' strength from them and into us, that would be amazing."

Ruby flexed her fingers with determination. "I can do it."

"And I can help," Darren said, standing beside her. "Use me for anything you need, Ruby. Drain the fuck out me. Whatever it takes."

I glanced at the sacred triangles we made. Three small triangles that came together to form a greater triangle of power. In witchcraft, the triangle was used for so many incantations that it was truly mind boggling. And here we were... three witches with three mates a piece, and with three spells that needed casting. I smiled at my friends. "Looks like this was meant to be. Three spells for the three of us."

Ruby smiled at me, her eyes shimmering with tears. "I always said we were perfect together."

"Mom always told us we were meant to be," Bella said, though her throat choked up on the words.

I clenched my jaw, struggling against the flood of emotion and the tingles of premonition tickling at my neck. "I love you both. Let's do this." I looked down at the spell book that was my task and summoned my magic to the forefront of my mind. My fingers pulsed with living power as I lifted the spell book into the air in front of me and stared at the timeless transcription with intense focus.

I read it over and over again, ready to cast the spell the moment I saw the bitch of a witch who'd cursed my parents—our parents.

Ruby began to reciting in the ancient language of the warlocks, calling out to the witch powers within all of us to entwine with our supernatural mates, and to draw their strength into our own bodies.

I began to ache and burn in the strangest way.

Behind me, my mates groaned and gasped. One of their hands dug deeper into my shoulder.

I didn't dare look back to see what was happening with them, I had to stay focused. Everything rode on this.

Bella began to glow with the white light of magic and power.

Her men stared at the ground with stony and determined expressions.

Tommy's arm shook as he gripped Bella.

I could only imagine the type of power an Alpha had—*and Bella has two of them!* The whisper of something akin to hope fluttered in my heart. We were really doing this! We'd succeed where our mothers had failed.

Then Bella began to speak, and evil was headed our way.

CHAPTER 24
TIFFANY

The chanting around me grew louder and louder beneath the cool winter sky.

Ruby recited the spell that dragged my mates' natural power from them.

I could feel their combined strength coursing through my veins like fire. Wriggling my fingers, I prepared myself to cast the spell that would stop Tabitha's heart the moment she materialized within the confines of our sacred triangle.

The air began to change, shimmering and rippling with white light and sparking with magical electricity. A person began to form in front of us, about our height, thin, and with dark hair. I could see through her as though she were a ghost. She was not quite material yet, but she was coming.

Bella began to speak faster, and louder as the spells wove around us.

One of my mates fell to the ground behind me; I wasn't sure which. But I felt the dip in my magical power immediately. Whoever it was, he groaned, valiantly grabbing my ankle a moment later. The power surged within me once more, like I'd been plugged back into an electrical socket.

The witch, Tabitha, became more defined.

I stared at the spell I would soon have to cast. The words stood out, highlighted against the page as if enhanced by a luminescent enchantment. I absolutely had to get the timing just right. I had to pinpoint the exact moment the spell would work on her, and I assumed it would be most effective and successful when she was almost fully here and present with us.

But she was fighting the spell, that was obvious.

Ruby was sweating, and her voice rose until she was yelling.

Tabitha faded in and out, like an old TV getting reception, then losing it again. She raised her hand and began to speak.

That was my cue. I had to act. *Now*. Before she flattened us all. With conviction I spoke the words of my spell.

She turned on me, glaring with evil, glowing eyes.

I could feel her spell trying to reach me—to touch me—but I held firm. I reached deep into the well of power my mates were sacrificing for me. Seizing hold of a power I'd never known could exist. I chanted louder and with renewed force.

Pain ripped through my belly and nails scratched at my face.

I put a hand to my cheek and glanced at my fingers. My hand came away covered in red blood. *That bitch.* Narrowing my gaze at her, I chanted harder, pushing every bit of energy I had at my disposal into the spell.

Ruby hit the deck opposite me. She was on her knees, barely speaking.

I could feel the well of power waning.

The groans and moans of pain from our mates had almost stopped.

Ruby's spell was scarcely holding up.

I needed to take Tabitha out. Now.

Tabitha was almost completely visible and wasn't anywhere close to being legally dead.

I glanced at Bella.

She swayed on her feet. She wasn't going to last much longer either.

I couldn't do it myself. I wasn't designed to do it myself. This was a team effort. We were all in or nothing. Without stopping the spell, I reached out each hand and called Ruby and Bella to me using magic.

They slid toward me on the grass, drawn as if with an invisible rope.

Their mates crawled or staggered after them, determined as all hell to stand by their women, their queens.

This was going to work! I reached forward just as my second mate fell to the grass behind me.

Bella reached desperately for my hand,

Then Ruby connected with me by grasping onto my fingers like her life depended on it.

I brought the book toward me. "My spell. Together. *Now*."

Tabitha fired toward me.

Bella flung out her hand and managed a shield of sorts that blasted us all backwards and out of the damage zone of Tabitha's spell.

I ended up on my ass, my mates sprawled haphazardly around me. "We can't lose! We're getting our parents back!" I cried out, surging to my feet. I grabbed my friends' hands and began to cast the strongest spell I'd ever cast in my life. With every word, I forced my power forward like a wave.

Bella's voice joined mine. It was weak but I could hear her.

Then Ruby joined in, whispering the words of the spell with everything she had left.

Tabitha fought me, pushing back against my magic with brutal force. She raised her hand to fire another blast of destruction our way.

I braced for the impact, but it hit me with bone-breaking strength, nonetheless, cutting my face and snapping my ribs. I cried out as pain ricocheted through me, hot tears of agony streaming down my face. *No. No! You will not win*, I screamed in my mind.

Tabitha's eyelids began to flutter and she moaned.

She's exerting too much of her own power, I realized. *She's weakening!*

That... or our spell is working! I squeezed Bella's hand and tugged on Ruby's fingers. The pain in my chest flared so brutally I wheezed. I closed my eyes as I tugged harder on my mates' power.

Tabitha began to scream and clutched at her chest.

I pushed more power into the spell, practically tearing it from everyone around me.

Then the sound stopped.

I opened my eyes.

She lay flat on her back on the grass.

Ruby climbed to her feet, quietly repeating the spell we all knew by heart now.

"Thirty seconds," Jase said from somewhere behind us, so quiet I could barely hear him.

I fell to my knees next to Ruby. The pain was so intense I struggled to stay awake. Black spots formed at the edges of my vision, threatening to blur my grip on consciousness.

Finally, after what felt like an eternity, Jase said, "Forty-five seconds."

I swayed where I knelt, uttering the spell one more time. Slowly and with purpose. Dragging crisp air into my lungs with each painful breath. It felt like there were a thousand needles splintering outward from my ribs, but I had to keep going.

"Sixty...." Jase whispered, then cleared his throat loudly. "Stop!"

And just like that I let go of the spell that I had recited a hundred times and gratefully allowed the darkness to take me.

I SWALLOWED HARD. I needed water. "Mom... I..."

"I'm here sweetheart. Here's a glass of water. Drink."

I struggled to open my eyes. "Mom? What happened? Mom..." I sat bolt upright, my head spinning, and stared at the woman in front of me. My rock. My family. My mother. "You're okay! What happened? Where am I?" I rambled in shock, confusion, and excitement.

Mom chuckled as she petted my shoulder. "We're home, sweetheart. Relax. This is your room and your bed. Though, I don't remember it being quite this big."

I grimaced. I'd forgotten to put my bed back to normal size after my night with my mates. "Oh yeah. Sorry about that. I—" Cutting myself off, I put a hand to my head, pain pounding behind my temples with a vengeance.

"Lie back on the pillows." Mom pulled a multitude of pillows around me and stacked them up so I could recline comfortably, remain mostly sitting up. "How are your ribs?" she asked. "And your head? I fixed up what I could, but there could be residual pain. Drink this." Mom handed me a mug.

I didn't ask what was in it. I didn't need to. This woman had looked after me since the day I was born and I trusted her with my life. "Thanks." I took a few sips and frowned. *Definitely a healing potion.* They always tasted like crap. I swallowed as much as I could, then handed it back, since my bedside tables had disappeared to accommodate my now ridiculously large bed. The potion was mercifully fast working, and a soothing effect soon stole over my whole body, making me sigh as the last of the pain in my head floated away.

"What happened, Mom?" I asked. "Is everyone okay? Where are my mates? Are the other moms okay?"

Mom sat down on the bed with me. "Yes. Everyone's okay, Tiffany. Your mates are all downstairs eating me out of house and home." She giggled, a sound I hadn't heard in years. "Lucky I'm a witch, or I'd go broke trying to feed those guys." Her gaze softened. "Thanks to you, sweetheart, everyone is alive and well. I am so, *so* proud of you."

I laughed. "For the weakest witch in the group, I did okay, yeah?" I leaned back against the pillows before experiencing a light bulb moment. "Hang on a second. Did you say 'everyone' is okay? As in…" I didn't want to say it out loud in case we hadn't done it. In case we hadn't succeeded in saving *everyone.*

"As in…?" Mom prompted, smiling softly.

There was a light in her eyes I didn't think I'd ever seen before, and

I had to swallow hard to stop myself bursting into tears. "As in did we break the curse? As in... is Dad...?"

Mom stood up with a big smile and took a few steps back. Then she turned toward my half-open bedroom door. "You can come in now."

A man stepped into my room so quietly I didn't hear his footfalls, but I could see him. Right there. In front of me.

"It's you." I swung my legs off the bed and stood up.

"Hi Tiffany," he said, his throat scratchy and husky, like he hadn't used it in twenty years. Which in actuality, he hadn't. He had light brown hair, shot through with silver. He had a wide jaw, my blue eyes, and was way too thin to be healthy. Mom was going to have to get some food into him, stat.

He stepped toward me, almost shyly. Then he met my gaze and smiled. "You saved us. You saved us *all*."

Tears burned my nose and my eyes. "Dad." I staggered forward.

He forward in a heartbeat, wrapping his arms around me.

I sobbed against his chest. "I've missed you so much," I whispered.
as

He held me tight. "Shh... Everything's okay now. I'm never leaving you ever again. Come here, Rebecca." He reached out his arm and brought my mom in for our first family cuddle.

She stroked my hair, a familiar and comforting gesture that settled my nerves and my fast-beating heart.

I closed my eyes and drank in the moment I'd waited my whole life for. I had my family together. Every pain and sacrifice, every tear and ounce of loneliness had been worth it. Our courage and unwavering faith in reuniting our families had finally paid off. And nothing was going to break us apart ever again.

EPILOGUE

TIFFANY

One day later.
Christmas Day.

There had been a bit of a fight over where Christmas was going to be held this year. In the end, Bella won the right to host our first ever family day. The new house they'd bought was even bigger than Ruby's place and could actually fit *all* of us together in the living room.

Bella had created a positively massive table. At one end sat our three moms and our dads, all cuddled together like hopeless, love-struck teenagers; holding onto each other like they were never going to let go.

Although I wanted to tease them for it, I almost cried every time I looked at my mom's happy face.

"Hey beautiful," Jase said, sliding into the seat beside me. "Does Bella know there's no food on the table?" He glanced forlornly at the pristine white tablecloth topped with festive decorations and new plates.

I laughed. "You need to wait and watch. This is a witches Christmas, after all. There has to be some magic!"

He huffed playfully and didn't ask any further questions.

I reached over the table to grab Ollie's and Fin's attention from where they sat on the other side of me. "Hey, I got word from my tenant yesterday, by the way. I didn't check my phone until late, but they're wanting to leave my house early in the New Year, so if you guys want to, we can get in and start painting, or knocking down walls or whatever, around the fifteenth."

Ollie grinned. "Hell yes! I can't wait to get a space where we don't have to be quiet."

I blushed and glanced down at the table. Since when were we quiet?

Bella stood up at the head of the table, Elliot and Tommy on either side of her. "Thank you all so much for coming to our first ever full family Christmas!"

Cheers erupted around the table as we all clapped and laughed with unparalleled joy. It'd certainly been a long time coming.

"I am thankful for so many things this year," Bella went on, glancing from one mate to the other. Then she slid a hand onto Jonah's shoulder, where he sat on her right. "My mates, my friends, my mom. But most of all I am grateful to finally have my dad back. Words really aren't enough to describe how much we've missed your presence in our lives, but know that we have *always* wanted you home with us and we are so grateful you came back."

I glanced at my dad, who had an arm slung over my mom's shoulders.

Our gazes met and he smiled at me.

My throat tightened and my heart swelled. I finally had *everything* I'd ever wanted. My mates. My father. And with time, hopefully I'd be blessed with a family of my own. A big one. With at least three kids—hopefully more!

Bella lifted her hands. "Ladies? Shall we feed our men?"

I nodded and rose to my feet, happiness filling me up like never before as I lifted my arms.

Ruby stood up just down the table from me.

And at the end, all three mothers joined us.

We began to weave our magic, creating our favorite traditional Christmas dishes.

Bella took care of the meats; summoning up enormous festive hams, pork with perfect crackling, tender beef, and succulent seasoned chicken.

I created a hearty deluge of piping hot rosemary and garlic roasted potatoes, with pumpkin and yams to compliment Bella's contribution.

Kathy and Sherie handled the side dishes, offering up loads of steamed seasonal greens, as well as a variety of gravies and condiments.

My mom made an array of sweet baked pies and heart-achingly beautiful desserts that deserved their own cookbook cover.

And last, but certainly not least, Ruby took care of beverages. and candy.

By the time we were done, the table was the prettiest thing I'd ever seen, and I could hear our mates' stomachs rumble around us like rolling thunder.

I sat down with a laugh at Jase. "How's that? Christmassy enough, now?"

He stared with hungry eyes at the table, practically salivating, then lifted an eyebrow at me. "Can you do fresh, hot bread rolls and butter?"

I laughed at his simple, wholesome request. "Of course!" I wriggled my fingers and created a huge breadbasket right in front of him piled high with rolls decorated by scored patterns and floral designs. *Perfect.*

"Just brilliant," he sighed.

Jackson stood and raised his glass of whiskey on the rocks. "One toast before we all get started on this magnificent feast." He lay a hand down on Ruby's shoulder.

She smiled and reached up to entwine their fingers.

"To our beautiful and strong Halloween witches. May they always love us, spoil us, and do amazing things to enrich our lives. From the bottom of our hearts, we love you."

I glanced at Bella and Ruby with a smile on my face that could rival the sun, unable to stop the tears as they flowed freely down my cheeks.

The men around the table all stood. "To our Halloween witches!" they cheered.

We lifted our drinks and then, together, drank as one.

I committed the moment to memory as joy swelled my heart. Our story would be passed down through generations of wolves, witches, and warlocks. Generations that would now be born and flourish because three best friends had the courage to rewrite their Fates.

THE END.

~

Thank you *so* much for reading the last of the
Whychoose Witches trilogy.

If you enjoyed this Fated Mates, Reverse Harem Paranormal Romance,
you'll LOVE my series: ***The Woodland Wolf Packs***! It's a trilogy of three
standalone romances, all intertwined within the same world.

You can download Book 1 for FREE:
https://books2read.com/the-packs-mate!
Or *read on* for an exclusive Sneak Peek into Book 1, **The Pack's Mate**...

~

CHAPTER 1

DEXTER

My pack's community grounds looked nothing like they did when I was a child. The once soft grass was gone, worn down to dirt. The area, central to our town, was littered with beer bottles and cigarette butts; the playground equipment long since hauled off into the woods by jack-ass youths.

The sun was only just rising, but we were all up, ready to start a long day's work. The heavy scent of testosterone filled the air. My all-male pack—consisted of Taylor and Jay, men with whom I'd bonded since we grew up together—

A sigh ripped through my throat as I glanced at the rock-strewn dirt at my feet. The pack before me was a powerful and depressing sight I'd grown tired of. For a whole generation now, the Woodlands pack had not born a single female. *Not one.* For almost sixty years the elders of my pack had questioned what happened to our breed. And what might happen to our genetic lines if there were no female mates to carry our children for future generations.

My mother and her sisters were some of the last pack-born women and each had produced at least three sons. What went wrong? To this day, no one knows. What we do know is that there will be no more children born to our purebred wolf-shifting women. It's impossible now. The last of our fertile females matured past breeding age almost twenty years ago; so, there's no longer any hope of a savior being born for our pack.

Something must be done. If we don't find women to breed with soon, our pack will become extinct. Great family lines that have existed beyond memory will die out and the world will be poorer for it. There was obviously only one option that remained... to bring human women into the pack.

We needed to venture into the cities and acquire human females for breeding. No one knows if the plan will actually work, as it's never been attempted before.

We have a unique pairing system called Fated Mates in our world. Wolf shifters in my pack only breed with their true mate, the one chosen for them by Fate itself.

I've always been told that I would recognize my mate by her scent. There would be an instant attraction, an undeniable bond from the moment we touched. I won't actually *know*, as I've never experienced it before. No one my age has. We must rely on the stories our parents tell us, which seem to change with time, just like myths and fairy tales.

So, what should we believe? It's tough to discern between the fact and fiction that has grown over the years. And if there were to be no more wolf-born women, would that bond still exist outside of the community? *Probably not.* We were in entirely uncharted territory and no one in the pack knew, not even the elders. And everyone was afraid of what would become of us if the bond failed.

"Dex! Come quickly. It's your dad." Taylor, my Beta, came running atoward me at break-neck speed and grabbed my arm.

My dad? "Where is he? What's happened?"

"Come on!" Taylor turned on his heel and ran toward my parents' home.

I followed behind, not thinking twice.

My father had been feeling unwell for months, and as one of the elders in our pack, that was a bad omen for everyone. They're meant to be the strongest of us. He can't die. *Not yet.* Not until we've secured the continuation of our bloodline. *I'll be lost without him.*

Taylor led me straight into the lounge where my father was laying on the couch and my mother was on the floor, kneeling over him protectively. His face was deathly pale, and his breath wheezed in and out of his chest like it took all of his energy just to stay alive to see the next moment.

"What happened?" I asked as I crouched down next to my mother.

Mom turned and squeezed my hand. "Please, Dexter, please. Take him to the hospital in Little Creek."

Little Creek was the nearest human town. "Mom, no. You know that's not our way. They'd notice he's not human. They wouldn't be able to make sense of our differences. It could endanger what's left of the pack."

We had a healer in our pack but he was rarely required for anything other than alleviating and mending fighting injuries. Our paranormal genetics meant that we healed extremely fast and rarely fell ill, unless it was something extremely serious or inexplicable.

My mom grabbed my shoulders with surprising force. "Dexter, you listen to me. I am not ready to lose him. Not yet. He can't die. Do you understand? Take him to a doctor. Now. *Please.*"

I looked toward my father.

He met my gaze with his own.

He didn't nod, but he didn't shake his head no, either.

And for the first time ever, I saw fear in my father's eyes. He didn't want to die. And just like that the decision was made for me. I had to take him in. "Taylor, grab Jay and the truck. Bring it 'round the front. I'll carry Dad out."

Taylor looked at me for a moment, as though questioning the soundness of my logic. But in the end, he followed my instructions as any good Beta would.

"Thank you, Dexter! Thank you," my mother said as she stood up and moved out of the way quickly, relief flooding her features.

I leaned down and lifted my father up over my shoulder, grunting with the effort. He couldn't assist in any way himself, so he was dead weight and he weighed more than me. And up until yesterday, he was still as strong as ever. Or so I'd thought.

With due care I arranged his arm over my shoulder and wrapped my arms around his waist so that I could carry him out to the truck. "Let's go, Dad." I didn't know if a human hospital could save him, but if there was any chance, then I had to try. Losing an elder would be risking the pack anyway, no matter how you looked at it. Mom was right.

I limped outside under the weight of my father's bulk. His ragged breathing echoed in my ear and his skin was clammy beneath my palms. "Are you sure this is what you want, Dad?" I asked a second time as the vehicle pulled up.

If my father didn't want the humans to help him, then I wouldn't force him. And I wouldn't do anything without his consent.

My father nodded against me, but just barely. He was growing weaker by the minute.

Okay. I was doing the right thing. It's what both my parents wanted. There was no arguing about that. "Let's go then, old man."

That earned me the briefest of smiles from my dad as I hefted him to the back seat of the full-sized truck.

Taylor helped me get him situated comfortably.

Then I climbed into the driver's seat. I adjusted the rear vision mirror so I could see my father's ashen face. "Little River is an hour away, so don't you dare die on us before we get you there, Dad." I bolstered my words with a threatening growl.

There was a weak laugh in the back seat from my dad.

Jay slid onto the floor behind my seat, at my father's feet, the perfect Omega. Lucky, we had trucks or he would never have fit.

My pack was in and my father wasn't getting any better just sitting here.

"Let's go." I planted my foot on the accelerator, and we took off toward the nearest town. I drove the roads as safely as possible, my heart thundering in my chest the closer we drew to Little River.

"Let's hope the human stories have been exaggerated, huh?" Taylor joked, trying to ease some of the tension in the truck.

The silence had become overwhelming.

I managed to smile. "Yeah, I think as long as none of us go shifting in the middle of the city, we'll be fine."

All of us of mating age ventured into the cities for clandestine sexual encounters with random strangers occasionally, but we never went anywhere near the heart of the city. Nor did we ever go to their hospitals or doctors when we were injured, for fear of the possibility of having our blood tested which resulted in them discovering a difference that they could not medically or scientifically explain.

We'd been told ever since we were kids how much the humans hated us. That they feared anything different, and that we'd be locked up in a zoo, or dissected on a scientist's table if they discovered who and what we were.

Taylor grinned. "Yeah, I hope so."

We drove the rest of the hour in silence, broken only by the chilling and unsettling rasp of my father's labored breathing.

Taylor pulled out his cell phone and directed me to the hospital using the maps feature. "Turn left here. It should be on our right."

The hair on my arms stood on end as we passed through the human city. *So much light, so many people.* There were a thousand shops and cars, and noise everywhere. It felt overwhelming. There was simply too much of *everything*. It was a level of chaos and cacophony we weren't accustomed to.

I pulled up outside the Emergency Department next to a hospital that stood a hundred feet tall. "I'll take Dad in. Taylor, park the truck and meet me inside. Jay, help me if you can."

Jay nodded and slid out the door easily, his agile, lithe body making everything easier for him.

I jumped out, opened the rear door and reached into the back seat for my father's heavy, but failing form. His wheezing was getting progressively worse. He was really struggling to breathe now, and his lips were a ghostly shade of blue. I pulled my dad along the seat, hard.

Adrenaline pumped through my bloodstream, making my muscles bulge and tingle with strength. My inner wolf instincts were telling me that time was running out.

Jay got under my father's other arm, attempting to alleviate some of his weight.

Then together we carried him toward the sliding doors.

They *whooshed* open and two men rushed out to meet us. "Do you need help?" they asked.

The foreign human scent rolling off their bodies made my hackles rise. I grabbed for my father's huge bulk, a growl ripping through my throat as they attempted to take him from me.

Taylor pushed at me. "Dexter, they want to help. Let him go."

Fighting back the red shifting haze was harder than I thought. *What am I doing?* I had to calm down, and fast. *Focus on Dad. Why you're here.* I gulped at the air and forced my arms to unhook their death-like grip. "It's my father. He can't breathe... I think it's his heart."

"We need a gurney out here!" One of the men yelled.

Another man in uniform came running up with a white bed on wheels.

The man who'd called for the gurney touched my arm. "It's okay. We're going to take care of him."

I helped them put my dad on the bed, my heart pounding with the fear and ferocity of my wolf as I struggled to keep him in check.

They wasted no time and wheeled him away quickly.

My father's skin was gray and sweaty, his eyes were closed, and he didn't seem to be moving at all.

"What the hell are they going to do to him?" I asked Jay.

He squeezed my arm hard. "Let's follow them and find out."

I walked into a human hospital for the first time ever and it was surreal. I'd spent my life in the woods, fighting bear shifters, and protecting my pack from outsiders, yet this truly was the strangest scene I'd ever witnessed. The fluorescent lights burned my eyes, and the stark, white walls stretched up before me and all around me like an enormous clinical maze.

I skidded to a halt before an indoor cage. The sign said *Reception Desk*, but it was a cage of sorts, nonetheless. *How do humans live and work in places like this?*

A woman approached us.

I searched my instincts. Despite the fact I hadn't seen a human woman in months, she did nothing for me.

Her face was too coarse and pinched. Her aura felt wrong and unattractive. "Can I get you to fill in some forms for the man they just brought in?" She handed me a black clipboard and a pen.

I nodded numbly and managed to relax enough to sit on an uncomfortable plastic chair with Jay at my side.

Taylor came running in the door, spotted us and took the vacant seat on my right.

It was the three of us against the world, as it's always been. We were pack mates; an Alpha, Beta, and Omega. Brothers, not by blood, but by a bond stronger than any other I'd shared.

"Whoa, I'd forgotten how hot these women could be." Taylor whistled as more nurses moved about and other patients staggered into the Emergency Room.

I shrugged my shoulders and focused on the human's paperwork. "You're welcome to them, Taylor."

The pack took turns travelling to town, hitting up the bars. Finding women to bed for the night. I'd always struggled with fucking women I wasn't connected to. Slaking my lust while still keeping my passions under control so I wouldn't hurt a fragile humans is not how I was designed. The Alpha wolf inside me craved the constant contact of my true mate. A woman to love and protect. Someone to complete me and bear my children.

"What's wrong with you, Dex? It's been months since we came to town. You must be horny as all hell."

I was. But I'd been running miles a day to keep the demons at bay. "I am," I admitted. "But I don't want any of these." I gestured to the room as a whole and glanced up again.

A young blonde woman stumbled over her own feet as she stared at us.

I rolled my eyes and kept my focus on the paperwork. "When my mate shows up, let me know."

Jay sighed. "We may not have mates, Dex. A real mate is a wolf shifter and pack-born. You know that's not our path. We're out of luck."

I looked over at my Omega, battling to keep my anger at bay, my gut burning at his words. "What is, then? To die without a mate? To simply grow old and be childless?"

Jay's mouth set in the familiar grim line he always adopted when upset. "We're still a family, Dexter."

"I know that." But still, I looked away.

A lot of the men in our pack were happy with their situation, but I wasn't. We'd grown up as one, huge pack, and at adulthood—at twenty-one years of age—we were ranked and chose who would share our own pack.

I was ranked an Alpha, of course. All three of my brothers were Alphas, the same as my father. As an Alpha, I was given the authority to choose a Beta and an Omega to complete my immediate family, my pack. I was lucky. It had been an easy choice. Jay and Taylor had been my best friends from childhood, and it felt perfectly natural when we built a house and moved in together.

But we were missing our mates, and despite how much I loved the guys, we weren't complete. There was a massive hole in my heart, and my life, and even if the other men didn't feel it as much as I did, it was still there. It was like a special, sacred piece was missing.

The receptionist returned to claim the clipboard full of information. Then we were left to our own devices for what felt like hours.

"What's taking so long?" Taylor asked, as he restlessly shifted on his chair, before he stood up, and began pacing once again.

We took turns wearing out the floor in the waiting area. There was nothing else to do.

I leaned forward on the chair and watched the white swinging doors that my father had disappeared behind. Over and over they opened and closed. And nothing happened. But eventually the doors opened, and a woman walked through. One I hadn't seen before.

I sat up straighter, my shifter rising to the surface. Who was she? And why did I suddenly want to take her in my arms and kiss the life out of her?

She was obviously a physician. I could tell that much by her uniform. She wore blue scrubs and running shoes that were well worn. She spoke briefly to the nurse and headed toward us.

I jumped to my feet, my heart pounding like I'd just run a marathon. and my skin itched and vibrated like my wolf was about to spring forth.

"Dexter Monaghan?" she asked, meeting my gaze for the first time, her sapphire blue eyes clashed with mine.

A growl rolled through my chest.

"Are you all right?" she asked, narrowing her eyes at my unexpected reaction.

Jay audibly gasped.

And Taylor went rigid beside me.

I could feel them reacting to her in the same way that my shifter was, which should have been impossible. We were meant to have our own mates. And she was *mine*. I couldn't explain it. I didn't need to. I just knew it. Maybe there was still some truth to those passed down stories after all. I turned to my pack mates. "Go, wait in the car. I'll be out as soon as I can."

Jay nodded mutely and began to back begrudgingly away.

But Taylor set his jaw. "No. I..."

I dropped my gaze away from my mate and stared at Jay, willing him to do my bidding. As the Alpha, my will was law, but I rarely exercised it. I never wanted blind obedience. I'd always firmly believed that bred insolence and contempt. I wanted loyalty and love. And that was earned over time. Then I focused on my Beta. "Taylor. *Go.*"

Together they fled as casually as their instincts allowed.

With that sorted, I turned my attention back to the woman before me. "Doctor...?"

"I'm Doctor Claire Masterson. I'm the physician treating your father."

"Claire..." I managed to say her name, even though all I wanted to do was put her over my shoulder and throw her into the back of our truck.

She looked at me strangely again.

I obviously wasn't behaving normally, and I didn't want to scare her off. *But how to do that?* "I'm sorry, Doctor. Please continue."

She straightened up, her throat working up and down as she swallowed hard. The woman looked almost as uncomfortable as I was.

Perhaps she feels this strange electric connection too?

"Your father had a massive heart attack. A cardiologist has been paged, and I believe they will operate tonight, inserting stents into his abdominal aorta. I'm here to give you an update and to let you know that there is a very good chance he'll survive and recover. You got him here just in time."

Thank you, God. Relief winged its way through my heart with such intensity that it robbed me of breath for a moment. I'd talked myself into thinking there was no way my father could die today, but from the look of this woman's face, it could have almost been a very real possibility.

My mother had said she couldn't live without my father, and hopefully she wouldn't have to. Not for another three decades or so at least.

"How long until he can come home?" I pressed.

She cocked her head to the side as if it were a silly question to be asking this early on. "Let's just take this one day at a time."

I ignored her human pragmaticism. She didn't understand what my father was, nor what his healing capacities were. "We live an hour away. I need to get my mother in to see him. If you could give me a rough estimate, I can let her know."

Claire hugged the clip board to her chest with a small grimace.

"Best case scenario, he may be home within two weeks. But he'll need to be managed by a local doctor moving forwards."

She didn't know that my dad's shifter genes would heal him as long as the doctors could repair the damage to his heart.

"Thank you, Doctor." I extended my hand to shake hers, my arm trembling with anticipation of her touch. According to the old stories passed down by my parents and pack elders, I would know my mate the moment I touched her. Now was the moment of truth.

Claire reached over and took my hand. Her gasp was as loud as mine.

Electricity pulsed between us like a thunderstorm besieged by lightning on a dark night. It would have taken out my knees if I wasn't so determined to stand.

Claire wasn't so lucky. Her eyes rolled back into her head, and she began to crumble to the ground like a falling house of cards.

I stepped forward and swept her up into my arms before she could hit the floor.

Her eyes fluttered as she struggled in vain to stay awake. She stared up at me with a confused expression, her eyelids dropping to half-mast. "What happened?"

"The mating call."

Her eyes closed upon hearing my answer and her body went limp in my arms.

I looked around. Not a single soul had noticed what had just happened. The waiting room was a hive of activity, and the medical professionals all seemed to be concentrating on their various tasks at hand and not the room at large. I turned slowly and began walking toward the hospital's exit doors.

"Excuse me!" I heard a woman call out behind me.

I kept walking, forcing my legs to keep moving, even though the scent of Claire made me want to kneel on the ground and thank the Fates for sending her to me. I couldn't stop or they'd take her away from me. I couldn't have that.

Once I got out into the fresh air it was easier to breathe and I sucked in a huge lungful. My head cleared a little and I began to wonder what the hell I was doing.

"Dexter!" Taylor called out from about ten feet away, having pulled the truck up near the entrance.

I didn't pause to think about it again. There was no time for reason or logic right now. I was running on instinct alone. I went straight for the truck with Claire still firmly nestled in my arms.

"Hey!" There were noises indicating a commotion behind me and I was pretty sure Claire's absence from the hospital had finally been noticed.

Taylor opened the back door without asking any questions and I put her into the back seat. "Step on it!" I commanded before I jumped into the back with her and held her tightly against me.

Taylor slammed the door, leaped into the driver seat, turned on the engine and fish-tailed it out of the parking lot like a real rally car driver.

I looked down on the unconscious doctor in my arms. She was a human and without doubt... my Fated Mate. *What the hell have I just done?*

~

Download 'The Pack's Mate' now:
https://books2read.com/the-packs-mate

www.ingramcontent.com/pod-product-compliance
Lightning Source LLC
Chambersburg PA
CBHW070949190726
48292CB00004B/1393